The amber eyes were haunting her, piercing her, eyes encased in a haze of black.

Suddenly terrified, Aileen woke from her dream as an equally terrifying sound enveloped her. Heart threatening to pound right out of her chest, Aileen sat straight up. What did it mean? Was it one of those dreams—inherited from her grandmother—showing her a piece of the future? Sucking in a ragged, shallow breath, she forced herself to focus. She was in her bed, not in the woods. But she still heard scratching at the door....

A branch, she told herself, willing her pulse to steady. But it didn't sound like a branch. It sounded like claws against her door, as if the wolf in her dream had taken form, following her into reality. She closed her eyes and put her hands over her ears, but the sound, muffled and distorted, continued to haunt her for what seemed like a half hour before finally fading away. She opened her eyes and finally stared out the window....

She was certain that something evil in the night stared back.

PATRICIA ROSEMOOR

WOLF MOON

HARLEQUIN®

TORONTO • NEW YORK • LONDON
AMSTERDAM • PARIS • SYDNEY • HAMBURG
STOCKHOLM • ATHENS • TOKYO • MILAN • MADRID
PRAGUE • WARSAW • BUDAPEST • AUCKLAND

ISBN-13: 978-0-373-88805-4
ISBN-10:   0-373-88805-8

WOLF MOON

ABOUT THE AUTHOR

Patricia Rosemoor has always had a fascination with dangerous love. She's won a Golden Heart Award from Romance Writers of America and Reviewers Choice and Career Achievement awards from *Romantic Times BOOKreviews* and she teaches writing popular fiction and suspense-thriller writing in the Fiction Writing Department of Columbia College Chicago. Check out her Web site: www.PatriciaRosemoor.com. You can contact Patricia either via e-mail at Patricia@PatriciaRosemoor.com, or through the publisher at Patricia Rosemoor, c/o Harlequin Books, 233 Broadway, New York, NY 10279.

CAST OF CHARACTERS

Aileen McKenna—Does the grad student go back to the Wisconsin wilderness to write her thesis or to discover her own past?

Rhys Lindgren—How far will the mystery man go to protect the wolves?

Jens Lindgren—What secret is Rhys's father hiding?

Valerie Gleiter—The current lodge owner has reason to fear more than the wolves.

Magnus Gleiter—Is the late lodge owner a dead man walking?

Sheriff Caine—Could the sheriff kill to cover up a secret of his own?

Madam Sofia—The psychic warns Aileen that all is not as it seems.

Fisk Oeland—Does the handyman learn too much?

Knute Oeland—Would he do anything to see the wolves eradicated?

Prologue

The full moon shone silver-blue along the earth, illuminating the tracks. He followed them to the snow-covered hillside where the prints ended at a dark maw that put a knot in his gut and fear in his heart.

Even so, he had to know the truth.

Taking out his flask, he took another swig. He'd been drinking half the night. Too much to drink meant too little sense, but he'd needed the liquid courage. He had to do this, had to find out for himself.

He had to go inside.

Tucking away the flask, he armed himself with a hunting knife in one hand, a flashlight in the other. His pulse *tick-tick-ticked* faster as he stooped low. Ducking his head, he quickly found himself in a chamber beneath the hill, large enough for him to stand.

He struggled for air as he flashed the light around the cavernous opening to be certain he was alone.

No movement.

No sound.

Nothing amiss.

And then he took a better look at the ground directly in front of him. The earth had been freshly turned. His limbs trembled as he got to his knees, and using his knife, started digging.

He didn't want to know…he *had* to know…

The knife proved ineffective, so he used his hands and dug like an animal, clawing the earth away a handful at a time. He dug fast, didn't falter until he uncovered the remains. A sight that seared him to his very soul.

He felt hot bile shoot from his stomach to his throat. The sour taste made him want to vomit.

He'd known…but he *hadn't*…

He needed to get out of there. *Now.*

Why had he done it?

What now?

Questions tumbled through his mind as he stumbled out from the earth into the night and fell to his knees. Handfuls of snow cooled off his face and neck and soothed the bitter taste in his mouth. He traded the knife for the flask, opened it and took a long swig.

The booze warmed his gut and made him feel

better for a moment. Until he heard a whisper of sound behind him.

A glance back gave him nothing, and yet he knew that was wrong, just like he'd been wrong to investigate alone. He knew what was stalking him. His pulse picked up, his heart kicked his ribs. He had to get out of there fast.

Flask in hand, he stumbled through the snow. The sounds of the night intensified. Panting, growling…

His mind was playing tricks…that was it…the wind, the crunching snow…

A low rumble turned into a howl.

He glanced over his shoulder as a dark silhouette rushed toward him. The flask dropped from lifeless fingers and he frantically searched for the knife he'd left behind as the moonlight gave the silhouette form and features.

"It can't be! No!"

Even as he shook in denial, he knew *it* was…

He turned and held out a hand…as if that could stay the attack…

Chapter One

Aileen McKenna got off the bus last, excitement and trepidation warring within her. She looked around at the small town of Wolf Creek, Wisconsin, the bright winter sun making its main street, barely two blocks long and lined with snow, glow with welcome. She knew she'd been here before—Dad and Skelly both told her so—but her memory of that vacation twenty-two years ago was hazy at best. Her gaze swept past the people and shops and the handful of homes to the dark forest beyond.

A man with a furrowed brow and narrowed light-brown eyes stood on the porch of the combination convenience store and bus station, his arms crossed over his broad, hide-covered chest. Though his basic expression reminded her of a scowl, Aileen knew he wasn't angry at anything. She grinned and headed straight for Donovan Wilde, who circled her with strong arms and gave her a brotherly hug.

"It's good to see you, Donovan."

"It's been a while."

"As much your fault as mine."

"When you move out here permanently," he said, "we'll fix that right off."

Aileen didn't see her half brother as much as she would like. He'd been raised in the nearby town of Iron Lake, Wisconsin, while she'd grown up in Chicago. But he was a McKenna, even if he did go by his mother's last name, and that was a bond that couldn't be broken. She and Donovan and Skelly might have been born to three different mothers, but Congressman Raymond McKenna had seen to it that his children were not strangers to one another.

"How are Laurel and the baby?"

Donovan's loopy grin transformed him from wolf man to husband and new father. "Both doing great. Laurel is a natural. And Willow is the most beautiful baby you've ever seen. Well, you haven't seen her."

"But I will, and before Christmas," Aileen assured him.

Other members of the McKenna family would be joining them for the holiday in a few days, the first time ever a McKenna family Christmas would be held in Wisconsin. Donovan and Laurel didn't know what they were in for when siblings and cousins and kids would descend on them.

The McKennas had rented out an entire B and B in Iron Lake to hold them for the three days they would all be here.

"I probably sound sappy about Willow, right?" Donovan asked.

"You sound like a proud dad, just as you should." She was aware at how thrilled her brother and sister-in-law were at finally starting a family. Laurel's first pregnancy had ended in a miscarriage, and it had been a while before Laurel had felt emotionally ready to try again. "Trust that I'm looking forward to meeting my new niece as soon as I get settled in."

"You could settle in with us. The invitation is still open."

Aileen shook her head. "You need to spend time with Laurel and Willow, and I need not to be distracted by a beautiful baby, or I won't ever finish my thesis."

The thesis was the final step in finishing her master's degree in wildlife ecology, a direction she'd been drawn back to after working as a massage therapist. She could thank Donovan— the original wolf man—for making her realize she needed to finish her graduate degree. Not that she wished to be a wolf biologist and be involved in research as he was. He was personally attached to the wolves under his care. He caught them and collared them and watched their progress as they expanded their territory over the years. Sometimes they strayed too close to civilization and got themselves killed.

Her interest took a broader turn—management of the wolves in the wild. She'd started the program several years ago, but had thought she'd made a mistake and left it. She was a city girl, she'd told herself.

Apparently not totally.

It had just taken her some time to come to terms with the decision that would change her whole life.

"I promise I'll leave some time to spend with you all, though. I mean beyond the research."

Though he no longer lived in a cabin deep in the woods with only a Franklin stove to heat it, he still kept his distance from town. Luckily his job required him to work in his beloved woods. Donovan would be a major resource for her thesis: "Can Wolf and Man Coexist in a Modern World?" She hoped to find out. Part of her personal research was going to be based on narratives from the locals in addition to those from the experts such as her brother.

She didn't see how she would get anyone to talk if she isolated herself as Donovan still did.

He fetched her bag and led her to a big black truck

encrusted with dirty snow. Winter in these northern climes could be vicious, but she'd prepared for the cold just as she prepared for everything.

Rather for everything she could anticipate.

What she couldn't have anticipated was the sudden angst being in this place gave her. Nothing specific. Just an uneasy sense of foreboding, of something being off.

Donovan slung her bag into the snow-packed back of the pickup. "Inside's clean," he assured her.

She nodded and, hefting her shoulder bag with her laptop onto the floor, followed it inside, grateful for the ride. A city girl, she was used to not having a car, to taking public transportation. That would have to change, though. She would have to buy a car for her job.

A moment later they were on the road.

"So how did you hear about Gray Wolf Lodge?" he asked her.

"Internet. I was looking for a B and B, but I couldn't resist the photos of the lodge."

The perfect place not only to write, but also to research some of her facts in person. She respected her brother's findings and opinions, but she needed to cast a wider net. The lodge was only half a mile or so from town—an easy walk for a woman who didn't own a vehicle and was used to hoofing it as far as she needed to in the big city.

Looking around as they drove, Aileen said, "Beautiful area. I wonder if tourism will be off, though, after that death I read about. Most people being afraid of wolves."

"The official report is that Tom Patterson had a heart attack."

"You think something else is going on?"

"It's not what I think," Donovan said. "Some locals claimed a wolf killed him. That's ridiculous, of course. Wolves leave people alone. But Patterson dead is another story. Animals snacked on his carcass."

Aileen swallowed hard. "So I read."

Once the truck turned onto a private road, the rough graveled surface bouncing the truck made keeping conversation to a minimum a safety precaution.

Their cutting through a stand of huge white pines brought with it a touch of déjà vu. Aileen wrapped her arms around herself to control a sudden shiver that swept over her. She'd never been here, not in this spot exactly, but the forested area seemed familiar. No doubt the family campsite that long-ago summer—in the woods not all that far from here—had been similar in nature.

Not that she remembered much of it.

After all these years, she still had a hole in her

memory, and no matter how hard she tried, she couldn't force her mind to cooperate. When her dad and brothers had taken her from the clinic, they'd assured her she shouldn't worry about it, because losing a day in a life was nothing.

So why did *nothing* still haunt her?

And why did the forest seem to have eyes? Aileen imagined someone—or something—was watching.

"Here we are," Donovan said, as they came through to a clearing that set them back to a different era.

He brought the truck to a stop in front of the lodge. Aileen slipped out and took it all in.

Built at the turn of the last century by Scandinavian craftsmen, Gray Wolf Lodge stood in magnificent three-story testimony to their skill. According to the brochure, the planked outside walls of the twenty-room inn were held together by square wooden pegs.

A brawny fortyish man stood on the porch. He removed his billed cap and threaded long fingers through a shock of pale hair laced with silver. Even though it was mid-December, the part of his face below his faded blue eyes was still suntanned. He looked fit, a real outdoorsman.

"Say, you Miss McKenna?" he asked.

"I'm Aileen."

He stepped down to the driveway. "Fisk Oeland. Here to take your bags."

Donovan handed them to the man who carried them inside. "You want me to hang around for a while?"

"No need, but thanks for the ride," she said, giving him another big hug. "Give me a bit to feel my way around. I promise I'll give you a call in the next day or two."

"Sounds good." He kissed her cheek and headed back to the truck.

"Give my love to Laurel and Willow."

"Will do."

She watched him drive off, then turned toward the lodge. Nothing sinister about the place, she thought, but going inside set her further on edge.

The common area, free at the moment of guests, was filled with rustic furniture and had cathedral windows and a high peaked ceiling from which hung a huge antler chandelier decorated with a giant red velvet bow. Strings of cranberries as well as lights and ornaments made from pine cones and others of colorful blown glass hung from the branches of one of the biggest Christmas trees she'd ever seen.

The tree stood between the windows and a wall-sized stone fireplace where a wood fire roared, watched over by several elk and deer heads. And on the mantel, a stuffed rabbit and beaver were frozen in unnatural poses.

Trophies, she thought. Someone's idea of sport.

Her unease multiplying, Aileen noticed a man in one corner using his laptop—the only other person in the room. She turned to the service desk built from the same stone as the fireplace. The thick counter was of fossilized wood. On it were lodge brochures different from the one she'd gotten in the mail. She flipped one over to find a photo of a blond woman with a rugged, bearded outdoorsman who, if his salt-and-pepper hair were any indication, was quite a bit older. The brochure identified them as Magnus and Valerie Gleiter, but Aileen was certain no Magnus had been mentioned on the Web site.

Fisk came down a set of stairs and crossed the room. "Bags are in your room already." He headed for a doorway behind the desk. "Mrs. Gleiter'll see to you momentarily."

She set down the brochure and removed her jacket. "I'll be fine." She would be fine. She was always fine. She always pushed past the things that troubled her. "And thanks."

Valerie Gleiter had been the one to reply to Aileen's e-mail requesting information about the place. The owner had seemed quite amenable, asking about her food preferences and whether she favored pillows and bedding of down or of a synthetic material.

Aileen heard a woman's voice, low and sharp, then a man's. She couldn't hear what they were saying, but Valerie and Fisk seemed to be in disagreement about something.

And then a tall, athletic woman exited the office. Aileen's eyebrows shot up. Dressed in leggings, ankle boots and a thick sweater with a fancy design, her long dark-blond hair pulled into a sleek ponytail, the woman looked picture-perfect for an après-ski get-together.

"You're Valerie Gleiter?"

The woman inclined her head. "Welcome to Gray Wolf Lodge."

Aileen's collection of loose Native American bracelets clanked as she held out her hand, then retracted it when Valerie ignored the offer, instead turning to the leather-bound guest register. Okay, not real friendly.

Though she'd had no preconceived notions about her hostess, Aileen was surprised at how young the woman appeared. But while Aileen was just finishing graduate school, Valerie owned and ran a substantial vacation property. She couldn't help but be impressed.

As Aileen signed the register, Valerie took her

credit card information and asked, "How was your trip?"

"Pleasantly uneventful."

Leaning closer as she returned the card, Valerie sniffed and blinked. "Nice perfume," she said, but she stared at Aileen for a moment, and her brown eyes flickered before she rounded the counter. "I'll show you to your room."

She swept by Aileen, a strong scent of ginger wafting along her path. Aileen followed. Odd that Valerie would admire a light woodsy scent when the woman obviously preferred one so bold for herself. Perhaps she was simply being polite.

"So how long have you and your husband owned the place?" Aileen asked.

"I'm a widow," Valerie said, her voice a shade cooler than before.

Aileen winced. Undoubtedly she'd stirred up feelings the other woman was trying to repress. And here she was simply trying to be friendly.

They climbed a short flight of stairs to one of the smaller rooms that fit her budget.

"Technically, the bathroom is connected to a second room to be shared with another guest," Valerie told her. "But you'll be alone in this section of the lodge. With Christmas right around the corner, next week will be a different story. By Christmas Eve, we'll be full."

Her quarters reflected the lodge, Aileen realized, with a headboard and dresser of rough hewn wood, fresh pine wreath splashed with a Christmas red bow on the wall and a braided rug on the floor the same rust-red and dark-blue as the coverlet. And if she wanted fresh air, she could go outside on a small stairless deck that butted against a century-old white pine. A chair there would allow her to sit and admire the spectacular view, which included the creek after which the town had been named.

"You're always welcome to use the great room," Valerie said. "If you want exercise, you can grab snowshoes or cross-country skis and explore the area on foot. Or take out one of the horses."

"That fits in with my plans perfectly. I thought this afternoon I'd get a little outdoorsy, check out the area on skis. Especially the part where Tom Patterson's body was found."

Luckily it hadn't snowed again since his death shortly after Thanksgiving.

Valerie started. "Why? You're not a reporter?"

Aileen shook her head. "Just a curious ecology student."

An awkward moment balanced between them before Valerie shrugged and said, "You know what they say about curiosity."

"But I'm not a cat," Aileen joked.

Valerie didn't so much as crack a smile. Apparently she didn't want to talk about the death. Instead she gave a quick rundown on the meal schedule and started to leave. Pausing at the door, she stared at Aileen as if trying to decide on something.

"If you do need to go into town," she said, her voice cool, "we can get you there. Or you could take one of the snowmobiles. The equipment shed is around back. Fisk can get you anything you need."

"Thanks, but I like walking."

"There's a shortcut. Follow the gravel road back to the main road into town. About a hundred yards down, you'll see an opening in the trees. A path has been kept cleared—"

"A walking path?"

"A whatever path." The owner started out the door, saying, "You can take the snowmobile that way, as well."

Aileen put the peculiar feeling she got from Valerie Gleiter to her own edginess. Though gracious and obviously successful, the lodge owner wasn't warm, not a true people person. Not that she needed to be, Aileen thought, glad to be alone. Sometimes she was too critical of others, expected too much of them. After hanging her jacket on a peg next to the door, Aileen pulled off her knit cap and poked fingers through her hair so it fluffed around her face and spread out around her shoulders. Now to make the room her temporary home.

Prepared as always, she opened her bag and pulled out the framed photos she'd brought with her. A few were of the McKennas—grandparents, parents and little kids—the others were of wolves she'd photographed while interning at a refuge the year before. Donovan had set her up with that gig. She lined up all the photos on the dresser so she could look at them if she got homesick, then trailed her fingers across the lifeless representations of the animals she both loved and feared. She knew everything about them. Their names, their diets, their health histories.

But she didn't know *them,* not in the same way the other interns and volunteers did. Even though she got physically close, a part of her kept her distance. Never one to let fear have the upper hand, Aileen had done everything the others had with the wolves, if with less confidence.

Would that ever change? she wondered. Would she ever be able to throw herself fully into her work?

Last, she pulled out a letter, the paper soft to her fingertips, the folds worn from years of inspection. The letter was her most precious keepsake, the loving legacy of a dying grandmother, who'd

wanted to pass down her promise of a great future
to each of her nine grandchildren.

> *To my darling Aileen,*
> *I leave you my love and more. Within thirty-*
> *three days of your thirty-third birthday—*
> *enough time to know what you are*
> *about—you will have in your grasp a legacy*
> *of which your dreams are made. Dreams are*
> *not always tangible things, but more often*
> *are born in the heart. Act selflessly in an-*
> *other's behalf, and my legacy will be yours.*
> *Your loving grandmother,*
> *Moira McKenna*
> *PS Use any other inheritance from me wisely*
> *and only for good, lest you destroy yourself*
> *or those you love.*

Both of her brothers and four of her cousins had
seen the legacy come true. They'd met their
spouses in the midst of danger—had saved them
somehow—and had made sacrifices to be with
them. Somehow, Moira McKenna, a *bean feasa,*
an Irish wise woman with psychic and healing
powers, had managed to pass pieces of her magic
down to most of her grandchildren, some more
significant than others.

The only magic Aileen had experienced had

been the ability to dream bits and pieces of the future. Sometimes she'd been able to patch them together, other times not. She'd never worried about it except when she dreamt of the wolves.

On her thirty-third birthday, Aileen had decided the wolf dream she'd had the night before was significant—her subconscious urging her to follow her dream and finish her graduate degree and start a new life away from the big city. As Gran had instructed, she would act selflessly in another's behalf—in the behalf of the wolves.

Aileen guessed her new life direction counted as her share of the legacy, though at times, she wished for a soul mate for herself. Too late, she thought.

She'd missed the deadline.

"Thank you for what you gave me, Gran," she whispered, planting a light kiss on the refolded letter and tucking it in back of her grandparents' photo.

After quickly unpacking, Aileen sprawled across the bed and groaned with pleasure.

Downtime. Oh, how tempting it would be to do nothing but relax and have fun this week. But she'd worked too hard to earn this degree. Now she was approaching the finish line for her master's in wildlife ecology.

More work awaited her. Her mind was already going over the facts.

Wolves in the wild didn't attack humans, not unless they were rabid. But there had been no report of rabies in this or in the surrounding counties in years. So had a wolf actually killed a man or was superstition rearing its ugly head, right here, practically in her backyard?

She would love to figure out what really happened, one way or the other, and include the facts and dissect the fiction as part of her thesis.

A thesis that explored new territory would help ensure her the job of her heart as a wildlife ecologist specializing in wild animal management.

The reason she was here. More specifically for the wolves.

Wasn't it?

AILEEN RESTED FOR A BIT, then decided to start working on that personal research. Dressing carefully against the cold and wet, she headed outside and around back to the equipment shed.

Fisk was inside, reorganizing equipment on a shelf. "Miss McKenna. Here to check out a snowmobile? Or can I give you a ride into town?"

"Actually, I was hoping for some cross-country skis."

"You planning on going out alone?"

"I have a map and a compass."

He made a gruff sound, then asked, "Where you headed?"

Aileen hesitated a moment, then said, "I wanted to check out the site where Tom Patterson died last week."

"You're awfully young to be interested in something so gruesome."

"Ecology student. I'm interested because I've heard a wolf might be involved," she said, as if that would explain it to his satisfaction. Not wanting to get into it further with the locals until she'd had a look at the kill site, she changed the subject. "You seem to be a jack-of-all-trades. Greeting guests, in charge of equipment. Like those cross-country skis."

"I do some of this and some of that," Fisk agreed. "I see to the horses and equipment mostly." Picking out a pair of skis for her, he glanced at her sideways. "But I do whatever the owner likes."

She didn't miss the change of tone at the last. Whatever. None of her business. Gathering up the equipment, she stepped outside and prepared herself for an adventure.

"Watch yourself out there," Fisk warned from the doorway. "You never know what could be stalking you."

He was staring at her in a way that made the

small hairs at the back of her neck stand at attention. Aileen ignored the sensation. He was just warning her to be careful. It would be nice if he'd more carefully chosen his words.

A quarter of an hour later—hood up, scarf wound lightly around her lower face—Aileen smoothly glided along a purposely carved trail that ran beside the creek for a while. She was in her element now. Pleasantly stuffed from lunch, she was invigorated by the welcome exercise and eager to get deeper into wolf country. Not that she actually expected to see one. Luckily for wolves, they feared people enough to keep to themselves.

Once the lodge was out of sight, she stopped and pulled out a copy of the map she'd gotten from a friend who worked for the Department of Natural Resources and reconnoitered.

The lodge was behind her, as was town, which was also farther west. The forest where her family had camped was situated a few miles north and east, in the direction of Iron Lake, where Donovan had grown up. And in between it and her current position lay a lot of territory, including the spot at least a mile away from the nearest road where the body had been found.

She continued along the creek for a while, checking the changing sky as she went. The sun had played its swan song for the day, hiding behind a bank of clouds, and a gray gloom settled over the area.

When the creek curved north, she checked her map again, then set off on a diagonal to the west. Not much farther. The past several winters had provided her with field experience, since she'd volunteered her time with a naturalist group that held wolf ecology weekends for high school students. So she knew how to follow a wilderness map. More important, she knew how to track an animal—a wolf—even though she'd never seen one in the wild.

The map showed a ridge and a downed tree in a clearing. Several minutes later, she found the site.

But where once the snow would have given up its secrets, now it was simply a quagmire. Even so, a thrill enveloped her at spotting animal prints in nature—even ones half eradicated by human footprints.

Crouching over her skis in the middle of the area, Aileen peered around, attempting to dissect the morass. Spotting traces of washed-out reddish-brown against the dirty snow, she sucked in her breath.

Blood.

Mouth dry and chest tight, she moved her gaze outward in concentric circles…until it met a pair of snowshoes lashed to a set of knee-high mocassins.

A nearby bird squawked and Aileen flew off balance. Her skis shushed to the side, sending an explosion of wet snow raining outward.

After landing hard on one hip, she stared up at the dark-haired man suddenly towering over her. He was garbed in fringed deerskin garments and wearing a head covering made from a fox skin with the head still attached. That and the rifle he carried made her stomach clutch. Pale brown eyes below slashes of eyebrow set in a rugged face narrowed on her. The eyebrows drew into a straight angry line.

Her stomach clenched in response.

"Who the hell are you?" he growled. "And what are you doing, sneaking around here?"

Chapter Two

Rhys Lindgren continued to glare at the woman as she defiantly launched herself to her feet, graceful despite the potential awkwardness of her cross-country skis.

Ripping the scarf from around her face, she gasped, "You scared the bejesus out of me!"

She stood several inches shorter than he—not that she was a small woman. No weapons on her person that he could see, unless the multitude of silver and stone earrings piercing her ears counted. Blond hair poked out from the hood loose around her heart-shaped face, snub nose and bow-shaped lips. One hell of a fine looking female.

"What are you doing out here?" he asked again.

"This *your* land?" she demanded.

"A question with a question?"

She crossed her arms over her chest and raised her chin. "I could ask the same of you!"

Because he sensed her defiance was born of fright, Rhys chose to use that to get her to talk. He stepped closer and lowered his voice. "Didn't anyone warn you it's not safe coming out into the wilderness alone?"

She blinked at him with eyes as blue as the sky in summer and took a short glide backward on her skis. "Are you threatening me?"

Without thinking it over first, he anchored a snowshoe on one of her skis so she couldn't move.

"Hey, stop that!"

"Who are you really?"

Now fear leached off her in waves thick enough to taste. Rhys forced himself to stay where he was, in neutral, with nothing but a snowshoe as his weapon against her. He held his rifle lightly, barrel down and nearly grazing the snow.

"Just let me go, okay," she said.

"Why are you here?" he asked again, looking around. "To set traps?"

"You think *I'm* dangerous? I'm not the one with the weapon. Do you see any equipment? Any traps? No! Look, I'm not here to start trouble."

So she thought *he* was dangerous. Good. Hopefully he could get the truth from her.

"Then why?" he asked. "To get a story?"

"I'm not a reporter." Sounding exasperated, she at last said, "I'm a wildlife ecologist."

"You don't work for the DNR." He was familiar with just about everyone working for the Wisconsin Department of Natural Resources in this area. They'd all been out here the week before, poking around both literally and figuratively. This one could be a new hire, he supposed. "No wolf killed Tom Patterson," he assured her.

He had his suspicions that it hadn't been a heart attack, either, especially since he'd found the body and a set of footprints that hadn't belonged to the dead man not too far away. Unfortunately, by the time the authorities had arrived, all traces of the sole's design—a circle with waves shooting from it—had vanished.

"I know it wasn't a wolf," she said. "That's why I'm here."

"Why exactly?"

If her changing expression was any indication, he had her.

"I'm researching the wolf-human connection," she finally admitted. "There's a story here that could be invaluable to my thesis. I'm actually a grad student in wildlife ecology. I don't believe a wolf killed anyone, not unless it was sick. But I realize not everyone is equally enlightened."

"And *you're* going to illuminate them? What

makes you think you can succeed where others have failed?"

"I can try. Do you find that offensive?"

Then a breeze picked up, brushing him with her scent.

Rhys started and released her ski. Though he was suddenly uncomfortable, he wasn't about to show it. And sensing she was telling the truth, he held out his hand. "Rhys Lindgren."

"Aileen McKenna."

Her reluctance was apparent, but she shook.

Even through two layers of leather gloves, her touch jolted him and he quickly let go. He trapped her gaze with his and tried to read her, but she somehow blocked him. Startled, he tried again, but again, she held him at bay. She was stronger willed than she appeared to be. He would get nothing deeper from her, not unless he gave first.

"If you're serious about what you're looking for," Rhys said, tamping down his frustration at not being able to control the situation—to control her— "perhaps I can help you. I'm well-versed with the wolf pack that travels this territory."

"You've actually seen wolves in the wild?"

Rhys laughed. Humans could live among wolves for decades and never catch sight of one.

"You would be surprised what I've seen over the years, Aileen McKenna." Those eyes—sky blue—it was as if he'd seen them before. He just had to remember where. "People in these parts are upset. Angry. Superstitious. Some try to destroy what they don't understand."

She glanced pointedly at his rifle. "Not you?"

"Protection," he said, gazing at her steadily. "But wolves don't worry me."

Aileen seemed to think over his offer for a moment. Then, nodding, she said, "All right. So where do we start?"

"My cabin."

Her eyebrows arched. "Um—not."

"We'll be well-chaperoned. I live with my father. He doesn't go out much."

"That isn't exactly comforting. Alone with two men I don't know? I don't think so."

"Then what do you suggest?"

"Gray Wolf Lodge. That's where I'm staying. Big fireplace…coffee or hot chocolate…"

"And chaperones not related to me," Rhys finished. "If that would make you more comfortable." With fascination, he watched attractive color flush her pretty face. "Tonight, say, nine?"

"Nine it is."

Having made the date, she skied off toward the lodge without looking back. The graceful way she moved transfixed him, and he couldn't so much as blink until she'd disappeared around a curve.

What was it about Aileen McKenna that had him tied in a knot?

Confounded by his unexpected reaction to her, Rhys stood there staring at the spot where she'd disappeared. Knowing it would come to him eventually.

THE STEADINESS OF RHYS Lindgren's gaze when he'd drilled her in protection of the wolves had put her at ease. Sort of.

Aileen paced the length of the lodge's great room as the hour of his arrival approached. Ten of nine and the place was already deserted of its few guests.

What—no after-dinner brandies or mugs of decaf? What kind of early-to-bed woosies stayed at the lodge?

Great. Here she'd been counting on backup and she was going to be left alone with a man who wore animal skins and carried a big gun!

Shades of Davy Crockett.

When Rhys had come up on her without making a sound, she'd felt somehow guilty for probing where she didn't belong. Besides which, alpha males always stretched her nerves taut. But his offer to help her had overcome her case of the jitters.

Until now.

Hearing a noise behind her, Aileen jumped and

then whipped around to face Valerie, who'd come out of the office.

"Aileen, can I get you something?"

"Uh, no. Just waiting for someone."

"Someone interesting?" Valerie asked, though she didn't really sound interested as she dug into a drawer at the check-in desk.

"Unusual is more like it. Maybe you know him. Rhys Lindgren."

Valerie's head whipped up. "The hermit's son?"

"Hermit?"

"Jens Lindgren. For years he mostly kept to the backwoods, coming into town only for supplies or an occasional meal at the diner. Now, not so much, and his son seems to be following in his footsteps. Although what they find so fascinating about being trapped in a cabin is beyond me."

"No one has seen Rhys?"

"Well, yes, but not often. Rhys mostly gets the supplies now, but he's not what you would call sociable, either. You say he's actually going to meet you here?"

"So he said." Aileen took a big breath, her senses filling with the pine scent from the Christmas tree.

"Interesting." Valerie thought on it for a moment before shoving the drawer closed and heading for the door. "Well, have a good evening."

Truth be told, Aileen was doubly glad she hadn't accepted Rhys's offer to rendezvous at the Lindgren cabin. She'd thought his name had been familiar to her. And now she knew why. Oddly enough, Valerie's evaluation of the Lindgren men reminded her of Donovan. She guessed there must be a lot of people in the world content to live their lives in nature, away from humanity. Rhys had said he'd been around wolves. Also like Donovan. She wondered if the men knew each other and if so, whether that would be in her favor with Rhys or not.

A few minutes later, a truck pulled up outside the lodge. She moved closer to the window and peered out in time to see a tall, dark-haired man slide out from behind the wheel. He wore jeans and a heavy black turtleneck sweater. No jacket. Then he turned toward the lodge and the moon silvered his familiar features.

"Rhys."

Not exactly what she'd been expecting after their encounter in the woods. He was…well…attractive in a rugged way…. Not that she should care when all she wanted from him was firsthand accounts of wolf interaction for her thesis.

Her stomach fluttered anyway and once he entered the lodge, taking a deep enough breath became a challenge.

"Aileen."

He uttered her name in a low, soft growl that surprised her considering how harsh he'd seemed earlier.

She responded in a breathless rush. "Thanks for coming, Rhys."

"Don't thank me yet. Your being in Wolf Creek at this time is a mistake. You don't belong here."

She jerked as if he'd slapped her. "If you just came here to tell me to leave town, you made a trip for nothing."

"You're not afraid to be here?"

Because of him? Maybe.

She swallowed hard and held her ground. "If you've said your piece—"

"I have nothing you can use for your thesis."

"Then why are you here? To bully me?"

Moving closer, he said, "Maybe to keep an eye on you."

So what was she supposed to make of that? she wondered, pulse jagging as the space between them narrowed. Obviously, he still didn't trust her.

Well, back at you, wolf man.

"I thought you said you could help me." Part of her wanted to move back, put some distance between them, but the stubborn part won and she stayed put. "Or is it that you've had second thoughts about cooperating?"

"Second thoughts. Third thoughts. And your thesis advisor would have some problems with the things I could tell you."

"Let me be the judge of that. Sit."

Speak, she wanted to say. But that might be pushing him a bit too far.

Rhys was staring at her, and in the dim light, the fire flickering, his eyes seemed to glow a rich amber like a fine whiskey. They roamed her face and he drew closer, just barely brushing her with his power as he moved around her to the seating area.

How the heck did he do that? Touch her without actually touching her? Somehow certain that Rhys Lindgren was no ordinary man, Aileen swallowed hard and followed.

He chose the couch and she chose the safety of a chair with a coffee table partially between them. No sooner had her butt touched a cushion than she politely asked, "Coffee?" as if there wasn't this weird undercurrent between them.

"Too late. I'm up half the night anyway. Caffeine would only make it worse."

"You don't sleep well?"

"I didn't say that. I just have unusual sleep habits." He didn't elaborate; she didn't ask. "So tell me about your thesis," he said.

"I thought you were the one who was going to

do the talking." Even though he now declared he had nothing to offer her.

"It would be helpful to know your slant."

His head tilted slightly and his eyes seemed to bore into her, as if he were trying to get inside her head. Did he still mistrust her? Realizing she was gripping both arms of the chair, Aileen let go and tried to relax.

Taking a big breath, she inhaled the pine scent permeating the room, then began. "I've been interested in exploring whether or not man and wolf can coexist in a modern world for a very long time."

"Long?" He laughed. "You're not that old."

"Kids can be pretty insightful," she countered. "I was always crazy about wolves and never understood how people extirpated them."

Her fascination with wolves had always been tempered with a trepidation she couldn't fathom— no solid basis for it. When she'd interned at the refuge, she'd hidden the fact by keeping mostly to office work and research projects that allowed her to study the wolves from a safe distance.

"And this fascination came from where?" Rhys asked. "Perhaps seeing a wolf in the wild?"

Her heart began to hammer, but she shook her head in denial. "No, nothing like that. I saw them in zoos when I was a kid and then at a refuge. My internship. Plus my brother is a wolf biologist who works for the DNR…Donovan Wilde… maybe you know him?"

Rhys shrugged. "I know the name if not the man."

"I'm very interested in the wolf recovery program. The fact that wolves found their own way back into northern Wisconsin and have thrived here fascinates me."

"Though it's still dangerous for the wolves. They're back on the endangered list, but that doesn't keep some people from wanting to see them dead."

She said, "At least *most* people in this century are willing to be educated about wolves and don't set out to destroy them. That's a positive."

He stared at her as if she were delusional. "You've been talking to tree huggers."

Aileen kept a smile on her lips when she said, "That's one of the reasons I'm here—to talk to people who probably put other things before ecology."

Rhys shook his head, apparently disagreeing. "You're here because of the recent death."

"That, too," she admitted. "You're the one who found Tom Patterson's body, aren't you?"

A few seconds passed before he said, "Unfortunately." Before she could question him, he turned the tables on her. "So which are you really here for? To determine the cause of death? Or to see the wolves themselves?"

Again her heart hammered and she once more gripped the chair to stop the fine tremor of her hands. "Both. Are you saying that's possible? Seeing the pack in the wild?"

"Most people can't, but some can." He shrugged. "I've studied them."

A thrill shot through her. Only a few people she'd heard of had been able to study a wolf pack. And yet, she had the oddest feeling…that he meant more than study…

"What else?" she asked softly.

"Isn't that enough?"

Somehow she felt there was more, but he didn't seem eager to open up to her. "So, does your father share your interest in wolves?" Is that how Rhys had gotten involved?

"He cares about anything that needs protecting."

Odd way to talk about his father, Aileen thought. "How did you do it, I mean the first time?" Her pulse picked up a beat at the thought of it when she asked, "How did you get close to the pack?"

Rhys studied her for a tense moment before saying, "It was shortly after I came to live with my father. I was restless every moment. Couldn't sleep. Couldn't eat. I felt as if something was wrong…missing. So I set out into the woods behind the cabin on my own, thinking I could find whatever it was if I tried hard enough."

He paused and focused inward and Aileen realized she was holding her breath waiting for the rest. "Go on," she urged. "Please."

"The deeper I got into the woods, the lighter my load felt," he finally said, a faraway expression softening his rough features. "A branch of Wolf Creek flows through those woods and I stopped to drink. I felt right at home there and relaxed for the first time since being brought to the cabin, so relaxed that I fell asleep. When I woke up, a wolf was sitting about a dozen steps away just watching me."

"The wolf approached you?"

He nodded. "A totally unexpected connection."

Aileen's pulse skipped a beat. Part of her knew how special such an experience would be, while another part was reluctant to actually do it.

Still, she couldn't stop herself from saying, "Take me with you."

"Into the woods? Not a good idea."

"It's a great idea."

"My opening a wolf pack to a stranger?"

"They need all the champions they can get. Call my brother. Donovan Wilde. You said you'd heard of him. He'll tell you I'm on the up-and-up."

Rhys stared at her, his amber eyes mesmerizing. She felt as if he were trying to get inside her, to read her. For a moment, Aileen felt as if they had a connection that went back further than that afternoon. Then she thought about going into the woods with a man she really didn't know…and her breath caught in her throat. The way Rhys was staring at her made her feel as if he were trying to get inside her head, the same powerful sensation she'd experienced out on the trail that afternoon.

Finally he let his guard down and nodded.

"All right. Meet me at the cabin at three tomorrow afternoon and we'll go out together. You have the best chance of seeing them at sundown. No guarantees, though."

Nothing at all could happen. Then again, something *might*. Aileen wasn't sure which she feared more.

"IT'S NOT TOO LATE FOR ME to call, is it?" Aileen asked when Donovan answered the phone.

"Laurel and the baby are sleeping, but I was up reading. What's up? Change your mind about the lodge?"

Aileen relaxed across the bed. "No, the place is fine. I met someone interesting I wanted to ask you about."

"A man?"

Hearing the teasing interest in her brother's tone, she said, "Yes, but not like that. His name is Rhys Lindgren. He says he can take me out to meet the local wolf pack tomorrow."

"Lindgren, huh?"

"You've heard of him, then."

"He's the one that found Tom Patterson's body."

"Right. I've read the reports. Do you know anything about him?"

"Only that he and his old man hole up in that cabin of theirs—"

"Kind of like you," Aileen interrupted.

"—with no visible means of support."

"Maybe they're wealthy eccentrics."

"They're eccentric, all right. The father moved out here after his wife divorced him. Then the son suddenly showed up. Guess he didn't want to live with his mother anymore."

"How long ago was that?"

"He was a teenager. Me, too, so count back. Rhys Lindgren never went to high school in this area, though. Maybe he'd already graduated. No one knows much about the Lindgrens. Like I said, they keep to themselves."

"What about the wolves? Rhys says he sees them, has studied them. Do you think he's on the up-and-up?"

"I don't know. Maybe I should come with you."

Uh-oh. Donovan was trying his overprotective brother routine on her. "Not necessary. I can take care of myself."

"In the city, maybe."

"How's this—I'll make sure he knows I told you I'd be with him out in the wild. You can protect me from afar."

Donovan grunted, then said, "I guess that would work. Make sure you take your cell. Call me if you need me."

"Absolutely. Now about that visit to your place. How does Sunday brunch sound?"

"Sounds perfect. I—uh-oh, the baby. I need to take care of her before she wakes up Laurel."

"Night, Daddy."

Aileen grinned and as she undressed for bed, forgot about Rhys for the moment and imagined her big brawny brother with a tiny baby in his arms.

That would be a sight to see.

I FEEL AS IF I KNOW YOU.

Aileen tossed and turned, part of her cognizant of being in that sleep limbo just before going under like a hypnotized subject.

Eyes found her...pale brown, glowing like amber...Rhys's eyes...staring at her.

They got inside her this time, traveling to all her

secret places, lighting her from within. Flushed with heat, she half woke and tossed and turned and shoved the heavy quilt to the foot of the bed before sinking back into her netherworld.

The connection was there, waiting for her and she sank deep into the drift where every breath, every heartbeat seemed shared with another. Odd that such strange sensations felt so natural. And then those sensations shifted.

Blood began to pulse sharp and ragged through her veins. Every inch of bone and flesh seemed to stretch and twist into something undefinable. Equally odd was the craving that threatened to consume her from the inside out.

What was happening to her?

Then the eyes…the amber eyes returned to haunt her…staring at her…piercing her…eyes encased in a haze of black…not Rhys…but a wolf…

Suddenly terrified, she pulled back from the image as an equally terrifying sound enveloped her.

Scratch…scratch-scratch…scratch-scratch…

Heart threatening to pound right out of her chest, Aileen sat straight up and out of the dream. What did it mean? Was it one of *those* dreams—inherited from her grandmother, showing her a piece of the future—or had it simply been formed through her disturbing encounters with Rhys?

Sucking in a ragged, shallow breath, she forced herself to focus. She was awake. She was in a bed, not in the woods. She was safe.

Scratch-scratch...scratch...scratch-scratch-scratch...

No dream this, but a sound coming from outside the deck door. A branch, she told herself, willing her pulse to steady. Had to be.

Scratch-scratch...

But it didn't sound like a branch. Truth be told, it sounded like claws against her door, as if the wolf in her dream had taken form to follow her into reality.

Scratch-scratch-scratch...

Hands over her ears to make the noises that followed her out of the dream stop, she yelled, "No, go away!" and curled into a ball against her pillows. "Stop!"

But the sound, muffled and distorted, continued to haunt her for what seemed like a half hour before finally fading off. Releasing her ears, Aileen opened her eyes and stared at the windows and deck door.

Certain that something evil in the night stared back.

Chapter Three

"Do you really think letting this woman into your life is a good idea?"

Jens Lindgren muttered the question from his perch on a ladder. Now he'd come up here for some book from his extensive library, but which? Senior moments—his life was filled with them these days, though he had a few months left before his eightieth birthday.

"Who said anything about my life?" Rhys responded. "I simply volunteered to take Aileen into the woods, where she might possibly get to see a wolf in the wild."

Jens looked down at his son, who was pacing before the windowed wall that faced those very woods. He belonged out there, one with nature. Rhys chafed in the confines of the cabin—at times he reminded Jens of a caged animal. It didn't matter how luxurious they'd made the place with the addition of more rooms and a library with an atrium to let in light and as much nature as glass would allow.

"It's a bad time," Jens muttered, suddenly remembering which book he'd been after. He grabbed onto the shelving to his right and pulled. The wheeled ladder slid him in that direction. "Too many bad things going on since last summer. Who knows what the McKenna woman could put together if she had all the facts."

"I trust her."

"You don't know her."

Ah, there it was. Jens grabbed the book off the shelf and, through Coke-bottle-thick glasses, took a look at the distinctive artwork on the cover— the outlines of a man and a wolf superimposed.

Descending the ladder with more care than he used to take, he glanced at Rhys again. Every time he looked at his son, his throat grew tight. He'd never known he could love anyone so much it hurt. Having Rhys here had changed his life. He'd thought he'd been saving the boy by bringing him home, but it had been mutual— they'd saved each other. After he'd lost his wife to another man, he'd come to Wolf Creek to die, but instead had found a whole new life.

He would do anything to protect Rhys from harm. Anything.

Rhys stopped his pacing and said, "There's

something about this woman, Father. I can't put my finger on it, but I feel like I should know her."

"Not likely," Jens groused.

Their gazes locked and Rhys tilted his head, but the boy was wasting his time, Jens thought. Nothing to read. He wasn't keeping anything back. He didn't know anything about this Aileen McKenna...did he? Another of many facts forgotten? Too many. His world was narrowing too rapidly for his comfort.

But if he did know of the McKenna woman, it would come to him. Eventually.

"She has an interesting thesis," Rhys was saying. "'Can Wolf and Man Coexist in a Modern World?'"

Jens blinked and focused on his son. The boy was taken with her. "You already know the answer to that."

He handed Rhys the book. The boy's angular face hardened, but he nodded and took it. Maybe if he read it, he would think twice about the McKenna woman and let her go her own way.

If he didn't...

AILEEN AWAKENED TO LIGHT flooding her room. The dream—had it been a memory or something generated by her grandmother's legacy or something real? Or a bit of all three?

She had to see for herself if something had really been at her deck door last night or whether her returning to Wolf Creek with its deeply buried memories had sparked her imagination. That had to be it. The deck had no stairs, no way for an animal to get to it.

Pulse ticking, Aileen climbed out of bed and crossed the room. Peering out the window, she saw nothing threatening, so took one deep breath, then unlocked the door and opened it. Still nothing. But when she connected with the door and jamb, her eyes widened. Ragged tears in the wood left fresh shreds on the deck.

As if something had been determined to get in.

Heart pounding, feeling as if she had a load of lead in her stomach, Aileen got dressed and went to find Valerie Gleiter, but the lodge owner didn't exactly respond to the damage as Aileen expected.

"The last guest who rented this room brought a big dog with him—some kind of husky-shepherd mix." Valerie kept her voice light and re-assuring, though there was a telltale quiver in her words, and her lithe body was taut. "The dog wasn't too happy about being put on the deck for some fresh air, so he scratched up the door and then ran away. Fisk hasn't gotten around to fixing the damage yet."

Aileen wondered if Valerie thought she believed the explanation. If it had happened weeks ago or even days ago, the scratches wouldn't appear so fresh. There wouldn't be curls of wood spread over the deck floor.

So what was Valerie trying to cover up?

Appetite gone, Aileen skipped breakfast and walked toward town, intending to get the lay of the land. The walk gave her the time to think about her plans for the afternoon.

Into the woods...

Why did that thought knot her stomach? She was in the woods now—pines towered over the road—and her vital signs were all stable.

Was it that she would delve deep into the mysteries of the forest...and her past? Or that she would be alone with Rhys Lindgren again.

Either was enough to speed up her pulse.

Deciding she wouldn't worry about it now, she pushed the image of pale brown eyes to the back of her mind and jogged the rest of the way.

When Aileen smelled fresh coffee and frying bacon wafting from the Cozy Café, her stomach growled and she couldn't resist going inside. The place was small, with a counter and a half dozen tables, all covered with red or green tablecloths. The other concessions to the holiday consisted of strings of lights lining the windows and ornaments strung across the front of the counter below the cash register. No tree here. A handful of people were eating breakfast.

On her entrance, conversations halted and all eyes turned to her. Simply because she was new in town or did they know why she was here?

Aileen smiled and said, "Morning!" as cheerfully as she could muster.

A couple of returned greetings and the customers went back to their food and private conversations and the waitress came to take her order—Liz, according to her name tag. Blond and blue-eyed, tall and statuesque, probably in her early forties, she was the picture of healthy Scandinavian womanhood. Her clear skin wasn't marred by makeup, but what she lacked in foundation, she made up for in blue eyeshadow and liner.

"Coffee, hon?"

"I'd love it, Liz," Aileen said.

She ordered a full breakfast, then confiscated a discarded local newspaper to read while she waited. By the time the waitress returned with her order, she'd scanned the thing from front to back. Nothing more about Patterson's death. So most probably he had died of natural causes, after all. Too bad the paper couldn't have reported *that* and cleared the wolves of wrongdoing.

Liz refilled Aileen's coffee cup, saying, "So I hear you're a student doing some kind of research."

Noting Liz hadn't mentioned the word *wolves,* Aileen said, "News travels fast."

"We don't have much to talk about in a town this size."

Taking the opportunity to probe a bit, Aileen said, "You've heard of that poor man's mysterious death."

"Damn wolves," a hard-edged guy muttered from a table halfway across the room.

He was a scrawny sort in a town of big men. Not that he was short, just gaunt as if he hadn't seen a good meal in a while. He had a shock of greasy light-brown hair and a full mustache carved down to his jawline.

Aileen said, "According to the report, Tom Patterson had a heart attack. You really think wolves killed him?"

"I know it. The only good wolf is a dead wolf."

The waitress protested, "Knute, please."

"Leave the wolves alone," Aileen said, trying to harness her instant anger, "and they won't bother you."

"Mind your own business!"

"Wolves *are* my business."

"You got a lot of nerve comin' here and stickin' your nose where it don't belong. Tom Patterson was a good man and now he's dead because of them critters."

The skin along her spine crawled and she wondered if it was attitudes like his that kept Rhys Lindgren from socializing with the locals. Still, she couldn't help but wonder what really had happened to Tom Patterson. Maybe she could find out, use the story as part of her thesis.

Behind Knute, a silver-haired woman dressed in purple velvet was tuned into the flare-up. And into Aileen. She smiled slightly, showing the gap between her front teeth, then nodded as if they'd made a connection of some sort and Aileen was supposed to understand what that was.

"Everybody keep calm," a uniformed officer of the law said from where he stood at the counter. His brown hair might be sprinkled with gray, but he was powerfully built, a force to be reckoned with. He took a bulging brown bag from Liz. "Let's not let tempers get out of hand or I might just have to arrest someone."

Aileen swore he winked at Knute, who dogged his head and dug into his breakfast chow.

"Sheriff Randy Caine," the man said as he paused at her table, his cold gray eyes fixed on her, shooting a thrill of something uncomfortable up her spine. "Don't you be starting no trouble around here, missy. We got enough as it is."

Aileen gaped at the man's back as he sauntered away and made his exit.

"Tempers are kind of easy to ignite around here lately," Liz told Aileen. "The town is already in an economic slump and rumors could hurt tourism, which is our livelihood, Christmas week being the big deal until spring vacation. Tom Patterson died of a heart attack, but animals did mess around with his body after he was dead. You can hardly blame folks for being spooked."

Again, the waitress avoided the word *wolf,* Aileen realized. "Are you spooked?" she asked Liz.

"Me, nah." But Liz didn't look directly at her when she denied it.

"This Tom Patterson—did he live in town?"

"No, but he came in regularly. Pretty social fella."

"So you knew him?"

"Ate here often enough."

"With friends?"

"You really are a piece of work!" Knute spat. "Patterson's no business of yours. Let him rest in peace and go on your way!"

Aileen figured discretion was called for and gave Liz a shrug that let her off the hook. Wondering what had piqued the old woman's interest in her, Aileen glanced back...but that table was now empty. Odd, the place was so small, you would have thought she'd notice if someone left.

As she ate her breakfast—scrambled eggs, bacon, potatoes and biscuits and gravy—she wondered about the old woman in purple. She couldn't put that knowing expression out of her mind, and so when she was finished eating and paying the bill at the register, she asked about her.

"That's Sofia Zak—Madam Sofia, she calls herself—a little touched in the head, if you know what I mean," Liz confided. "The story is that she used to work in carnivals telling fortunes, but then she married a local shopkeeper and settled down here in Wolf Creek. She's a widow now. She owns Caravan Herbs and Potions down at the far end of Pine Street."

"Thanks," Aileen said, tipping the waitress extra.

Leaving the café, she wandered down Main Street, which was decorated with swags of pine and red ribbons at every lamppost. The shop windows were similarly decorated. Patterson's death could keep tourists away, Aileen realized, which could bankrupt a shopkeeper on the edge.

Her thoughts gravitated back toward Rhys and the outing she would share with him that afternoon. As much as Rhys had tried to put her off, she felt a bond with him beyond simple attraction. Had to do with their love of wolves, she guessed. Knute's behavior in the diner made her appreciate Rhys all the more. Trying to get her mind off him for the moment, though, she checked out the displays in the shop windows, but nothing interested her.

No herbs. No potions. No Madam Sofia.

She found herself gravitating to Pine Street and eventually to Sofia Zak's business. A sign amongst the bunches of dried plants hanging in the window indicated Madam Sofia still read palms.

Raising her eyebrows, Aileen went inside.

The shop was dimly lit and her eyes took a moment to adjust. Cloth draped from the ceiling in long swaths gave the place the feel of a tent. Like a fortune-telling tent? The first object that came into focus was a stuffed bird—a predator posed with wings outspread, neck arched, beak open, as if it were protecting the shop.

Pulse surging at her own whimsy, Aileen called out, "Madam Sofia?"

While there was no answer, she heard movement from the back room. Then a hand parted the strings of beads hanging in the doorway to the back. Madam Sofia followed.

"I knew you would come."

Again, Aileen raised her eyebrows. That smile

had been knowing. Is that how she lured new customers to her shop? Did they come here out of simple curiosity?

"I'm just wandering around trying to get better acquainted with Wolf Creek. Your shop looked interesting."

"That's not why you're here. You want the information I can give you."

Aileen grinned. "How can you be sure?"

"You're very unsettled. You don't like being here, and yet you need something you can get nowhere else. Reassurance of some kind."

Though her grin faded, Aileen tried to laugh it off. "Good guess. That could fit anyone trying to work out a problem, which, of course, most people have enough of to make your guess probable."

"Ah, well, either you believe or you don't. Perhaps I can interest you in my physical wares."

Aileen looked over a display of hair and skin products and chose a bottle of herbal shampoo that had a woodsy smell she liked.

As she was paying for the product, she said, "This place is called Caravan Herbs and Potions. What kind of potions?"

She expected the answer to be love potions or cold remedies or some such.

"It depends on what you need." When Aileen

didn't say anything, the old woman added, "For you, a protection spell would be wise." That knowing smile once more curved Madam Sofia's lips. "Against werewolves."

"Uh-huh."

Obviously the word that she was interested in wolves had already gotten around, and the woman was twisting the information to scare her and to make another sale.

"You don't believe me now, but you will," Madam Sofia predicted. "Tom Patterson died under the last full moon. I can tell you things that would curl your hair. Come back to me for protection before it's too late."

Definitely uneasy now, Aileen took her package and headed for the door. The woman was either mentally ill or a master at getting people to buy worthless potions.

"You have a good afternoon," she said, glancing back.

Once more, Madam Sofia had melted into the ether.

"She said she'd be gone all day," Valerie told Fisk as they entered Aileen's room. "I was hoping you could take care of the damage before she got back."

"I'll see what I can do."

Fisk came up behind her as she unlocked the deck door. She felt his heat as surely as if he were touching her. Every nerve stirred inside her, but she wouldn't act on it, not here, not in the room Magnus had favored.

Their quarters had been downstairs, adjoining the office, but when he'd wanted to have her, he'd taken her here, to this room away from the others where no one would hear them. Magnus had been a very demanding and noisy lover. The private deck had been added incentive to use these quarters. When he'd had the mind for it, they'd coupled out there, no matter the weather or temperature.

Thinking about his inventiveness and stamina sharpened the desire filling her. Bedding him was the only thing she missed about her late husband.

Opening the door, Valerie said, "There, see," and pointed to the destruction.

"What the hell!" Fisk squatted and fingered the wood shavings, then rubbed his hand along the jamb the way she wanted him to rub her. "I don't understand. This is the second time in less than two weeks."

"Some animal searching for food," she murmured.

"How an animal got up here is the question."

Not wanting Fisk to ask too many questions—

ones Valerie didn't want to think on too closely—
she edged closer. "I want you," she murmured.

"Now?" he asked, his sun-bronzed features
taking on that edge she so appreciated in him as a
lover.

He pulled her to him roughly and kissed her.
For a moment, Valerie caved and with a moan,
melted against him and rubbed her breasts against
his chest. Such sweet torture. How she hated to
stop him. But she had to.

She shoved against Fisk's chest, saying, "Soon.
As soon as you finish here, come to me."

He grunted but didn't argue.

Valerie slipped one leg over the railing and
rubbed herself against the polished wood. As
though he could smell her heat, Fisk cursed softly
and stepped toward her, but Valerie laughed—it was
only a tease to make him hurry—and swung the
other leg over. Aiming for a soft spot, she dropped
to the snow-covered ground and took off at a lope
for her cabin she'd had built into the side of a hill.

Now Fisk would work fast, his mind on her
rather than on an explanation as to what was going
on with some wild animal wanting to get inside the
house.

And she would be waiting for the workman,
Valerie thought, picturing herself naked on the
bearskin rug in front of a roaring fire. He would

take her roughly and fast, the way a man like that was wont to do. The way she liked it.

Again she was reminded of her late husband.

And of those damn claw marks.

But she refused to believe that Magnus had come back from the dead.

Chapter Four

Barreling toward the Lindgren cabin on a snowmobile, whose noisy engine split the quiet, Aileen wondered what it would take to stir her enthusiasm for personal research. She'd come to Wolf Creek for the quiet, for the atmosphere, for the people with their strong opinions.

She hadn't come to lose herself in the woods.

A shiver crept along her spine at the thought of being lost out there. But that couldn't happen with Rhys playing guide, she assured herself. The really scary part of this venture was the possibility of meeting a wild wolf nose-to-nose. Even Rhys himself wasn't that scary.

She came around a bend and stopped on a hill with a view of the Lindgren cabin—if you could still call it that, considering the two-story addition to the original structure. Though surrounded by forest, the place looked big enough to house a family with several kids. A couple of bachelors would undoubtedly rattle around in all that room.

Knowing Rhys would be waiting for her, Aileen ignored the knot in her stomach and headed the snowmobile toward the front door. As she swept down a gentle incline, she saw a man too small to be Rhys by the woodpile. That must be his father, Jens, then. Arms stacked with wood, Jens turned to face her as she slowed the vehicle in a cleared area where the truck and a pair of snowmobiles were parked.

Leaving her vehicle and moving toward the man, Aileen noted how much older he looked than she'd expected—white hair, face weathered and deeply creased by the outdoors—but the really odd thing was that he didn't have a thing in common with Rhys. Behind thick glasses, his eyes were a pale blue. And his features were softer, more rounded. Rhys must resemble the other side of the family, Aileen decided, wondering if he ever saw his mother.

Jens moved toward the door, and as she joined him, he studied her as if he were taking her measure. "You're the McKenna woman."

"I am, but you can call me Aileen." When he didn't relax his stance, she asked, "Is there something the matter, Mr. Lindgren?"

"I'm trying to decide. I hope not."

"I don't understand."

"You're a danger here," he said, then abruptly turned away from her and opened the door. "Go on in."

Frowning, she wondered what he meant by that. He hadn't said *in* danger. He'd said *a* danger, as if she were bringing them trouble.

After stomping the snow off his boots, Jens crossed the room and dropped the armload of wood in a box next to the fireplace. Aileen unwound her scarf and opened her jacket. The room was toasty warm. It was also very masculine with a lot of wood—both structure and furniture—much like the great room at the lodge. But unlike the lodge, there was no evidence of stuffed animals here. Also unlike the lodge, the Christmas tree was still alive, a smallish fir in a planter that sat in front of the windows.

Would they plant it when spring came? she wondered, liking the idea of having a tree one didn't have to kill to enjoy.

"The boy's in the library," Jens said, indicating the open door at the far wall.

Realizing he meant for her to find her own way, she said, "Thank you," and then felt the man's eyes follow her every inch of the way.

Removing her jacket as she entered the library, Aileen caught her breath at the sight before her.

One wall was all windows, while the other was all shelves that rose to the ceiling, which had to be fifteen feet high. She'd never seen so many books in a private collection. There had to be thousands of them. One of which had Rhys's full attention.

He sat in one of two plaid club chairs by the windows with their incredible view, his long legs and stockinged feet stretched out in front of him. She imagined he and Jens spent hours here keeping each other quiet company while absorbed in their books. Whatever Rhys was reading now held him in thrall, for he didn't seem to realize she was in the room.

Taking advantage of the opportunity, she studied him for a moment.

His expression intent, he seemed to be absorbing the information as if the content was important to him. His body encased in tight jeans and a thin turtleneck…well-honed muscles beneath the material spelled raw power. His fingers dragging across the page…they were unusually long, especially the ring and middle finger, which were both the same length.

Then those fingers stopped moving and drummed a beat on the page, as if Rhys were taking particular note of some specific information.

What had him so engrossed? Aileen wondered, stepping closer to find out.

Before she got so much as a peek, Rhys snapped the book shut and caught her with his gaze. His intensity quickly swelled—impossible to ignore—as if he were trying to climb inside her the way he had out on the trail the day before. She could literally feel the heightened awareness pouring out of him and into her until she avoided his eyes.

At which, he said, "You're early."

"I thought to come before I changed my mind again, but since you're busy," she said, starting to back away, "I'll leave you alone and—"

Rhys fastened those fingers around her wrist. "No."

His grip was light, but as secure as a handcuff. She could feel his pulse as if it were her own, reminding her of the dream she'd had in the middle of the night. Suddenly she found she was squeezing her jacket to her breast, as though she could slow the rapid beat of her heart.

"You can let go now," she choked out. "I won't leave. I was trying to be considerate."

"You're afraid."

"Oh, please."

Rhys cocked his head and studied her. "Your eyes are dilated, your breathing is shallow, your heartbeat accelerated."

"Now you *are* making me nervous."

She dropped her gaze to the fingers still holding her captive and they suddenly released her and she could take a deep breath again.

Aileen glanced back to his book, but before she could see one word of the contents, Rhys slammed it closed. The wolf and man on the cover immediately drew her attention, made her believe the contents contained information on wolf-human connections, which might be useful for her thesis.

"I don't think I know that one," she said.

Rhys put the book aside on the table and rose. "The real thing is much more interesting than anything you can find in a book." One thick, straight eyebrow rose as he stared at her, seemingly in challenge, a knowing smile curving his mouth.

"Do you mean the wolves or you?"

"Take your pick."

"Let's go with the wolves," she said, trying to stay on topic. "They're why I'm here."

He gave her one of those white-toothed grins. "If you say so."

Heat burned her cheeks as she followed him out of the room. She couldn't deny she found him attractive, but he didn't have to amuse himself at her expense.

At the fireplace, poker in hand, Jens turned and stiffly asked, "You're going, then?"

"As soon as I change," Rhys said. "In the meantime, can you entertain Aileen for me?"

Jens turned back to stoke his fire. Right, he was certainly entertaining.

Aileen walked over to the window. More forest. Everywhere she looked, there was more forest. A sliver of apprehension returned and a knot tightened her stomach. She didn't have to go anywhere to confront her fear—she was in the woods now.

"Rhys is special," Jens suddenly told her.

She'd felt that herself, but she hadn't exactly been able to put words to it. Maybe he could. "Special how?"

"He's one with nature."

"Then I should be able to enrich my thesis by picking his brain."

"You can destroy him."

The second time Jens had said something negative about her influence. First it was *danger,* now *destroy.* "I don't understand. How?"

"By making him want something he can't have."

Before she could quiz him further on what exactly that might be, a door opened and Rhys said, "Ready."

Garbed in deerskin pants and knee-high moccasins and a heavy sweater, Rhys grabbed his fringed jacket and what looked like a water bottle in a leather covering from a peg by the door.

"Don't be late," Jens said, heading for the library. "Be back before dark."

"That won't be a problem tonight," Rhys said, tone soothing.

Jens grunted in what sounded like his continued disapproval and disappeared through the doorway.

Slipping back into her jacket and throwing the scarf around her neck, Aileen eyed the fox headgear still hanging from a peg. She didn't get it—Rhys wanted to protect wolves, but he would hunt a fox? Even as she thought it, he picked one of the two rifles off the wall rack above the clothing pegs.

Uncomfortable, she asked, "Do you have to wear that headgear?"

"I wasn't planning on it. It's too warm today."

Warm enough that the snow was melting. Hopefully not enough to turn everything to slush or riding on the snowmobile would turn out to be less than pleasant. But it seemed Rhys had no intention of taking vehicles.

"The noise would be sure to scare off the wolves," he assured her as they stepped outside.

From a box on the stoop, he fetched snowshoes with hide lacings and handed her a pair. Now why couldn't he have picked skis? She'd never gotten the hang of tromping around comfortably in snow-shoes.

"If I kill myself on these…"

"Don't worry, I'll bury you deep," he promised, his tone mocking. "No wolves will snack on you."

Great. He had to plant that in her mind now.

He started off, saying, "Now walk like a wolf."

Following, she grumbled, "I'd like to see a wolf walk in snowshoes."

But she knew what he meant. A pack of wolves on the move stepped in the leader's footprints. Often, unless you looked close, it appeared that only one wolf had gone by. Her walking in his prints made negotiating the melting snow a little easier on her.

Within a quarter of an hour, she was moving along without a hitch and her endorphins had kicked in. And she was warm enough to untie her scarf and unzip her jacket, both in front and under the arms to open the vents.

"You should wear leather," Rhys said. "More comfortable when you work up a sweat."

"It's not my jacket that's the problem," she said with a breathless gasp. "Your legs…simply longer than mine…have to work to keep up."

"Why didn't you say I was pushing too fast?" he asked, immediately slowing.

"Trying to be macho," she joked.

Just ahead, there was a small clearing with a couple of fallen logs. Rhys led her there and made her sit so she could catch her breath. He handed her the water bottle, then set down his rifle and searched the ground behind her for something.

"Looking for tracks?"

"Too soon," he said. "Not that the pack doesn't come close to the cabin. But that's usually in the middle of the night."

"And you know this how?"

"I told you I wake frequently. And the wolves howl."

Calling him? she thought.

A wolf howling in the wild...

A little chill shot down her spine. She could almost hear the echo in her head. Now where did that come from? It had to be a memory, yet she couldn't place it.

A sturdy tree branch in hand, Rhys sat next to her.

"Going to build a fire?"

"Going to make you a staff," he said, pulling a knife he'd strapped to his moccasins.

"You come prepared."

"You never know what you might run into out here."

Another shiver. What had happened to her in

the woods? What had happened to Tom Patterson?

Rhys quickly stripped the branch of any offshoots. Fascinated, Aileen watched him work.

His hands were sure, as if he'd done this hundreds of times. She could imagine those hands working on her, stripping off her clothes, smoothing her skin...

Rhys glanced up and heat seared her cheeks.

"You certainly took to the outdoors," she said, trying to cover. "Your father was a good teacher."

"That he was. He taught me everything I know. He didn't just teach me to be self-sufficient. Actually, he used to be a college professor. Psychobiology," he added, "studying the interactions between biology and behavior. Father made sure I was properly educated."

"You didn't go to school?"

"Didn't need to. Everything I needed to learn is in our library. Literature. History. Sciences. Everything. My knowledge is equivalent to an advanced degree. Father gave me my love for learning."

Which she'd seen firsthand, Aileen thought, remembering the book he'd been reading when she'd come in. He'd been totally engrossed in the pages.

"It sounds as if you've read a lot of those books

in your library. But didn't you miss being with other teenagers while you were growing up?" she asked. "Actually, how about being with people in general?"

"I had the wolves." Rhys handed her a very sturdy staff. "This might come in handy when the trail gets rough."

"Thanks." She stood. "I'm good to go."

This time they started out side by side. The deeper into the woods they traveled, the narrower the path between pines, the shallower the snow, the less use for the staff to make walking easier. Still, Aileen appreciated Rhys's gesture in seeing to her comfort.

"So what about you," he said. "Where and who you come from."

"My family has always lived in Chicago. I had a traditional education and as you know, I'm still at it. I have two brothers—Skelly and Donovan. As I said, Donovan lives not too far from here. I told him about our excursion today."

"What did he say?"

"To be careful."

Rhys's eyebrows pulled together in a dark V. "The only danger you need to watch for would be from other humans."

A few minutes later, Rhys took the lead again, and Aileen noticed a subtle shift in his posture. His back seemed straighter, and he appeared to be more alert, head constantly turning, as if he were on guard, watching for something. The wolves, she assumed. Then he stopped suddenly, lifted his head and sniffed the air.

Nearly crashing into him, she gasped, "Is something wrong?"

"Fire."

Aileen took a whiff. Nothing.

But Rhys cursed under his breath and moved off the trail and straight through the trees. He kept going without looking back.

Pulse racing, Aileen followed, her awkwardness on the snowshoes slowing her down. Ahead, Rhys stopped and lowered himself to his haunches, and as she came up behind him, she saw the fire ring that indicated someone had camped here.

But the contents looked cold, so how in the world had Rhys smelled the ash?

"Hunters," he said.

His gaze roamed the area around them and his visage went dark, alarming Aileen. She didn't know why Rhys seemed so incensed. He stood stiffly as if he were frozen. His anger scared her a little as did an awareness of some invisible power that suddenly rippled off him in waves.

As if spotting what he was looking for, Rhys took off again without a word, leaving her to keep up the best way she could.

"Hey, wolf man, wait for me!"

The snow wasn't particularly deep, but the ground was uneven, making it slow going for her. By the time she caught up to Rhys, he was on his haunches again, his back to her. It wasn't until she stood over him that she could see what he'd found—a baited leghold trap.

"Oh, no," she murmured.

"Damn wolf haters!" he gnarled, his reaction dark and intense. He wedged a chunk of rock between the steel jaw so it couldn't snap on him. He removed the meat and smelled it, and his expression darkened. "Poisoned!"

How in the world would he know that? she wondered, asking, "What can we do?"

As if his fury kept him from hearing her, Rhys kept his gaze on the weapon of destruction. First he removed the rock, his movement unbelievably fast. The jaw snapped shut, giving her gooseflesh. Then, from inside his jacket, Rhys pulled a hatchet and with one powerful whack brought the blade down on the hinge and destroyed it. With the trap in two pieces, he threw each half in a different direction, sending them sailing into oblivion.

Aileen watched in awed silence. Rhys's adrenaline rush had made him even faster and stronger than usual.

"Gather some rocks," he told her.

Then using the hatchet again, Rhys cut into the solid earth while Aileen did as he ordered. When her arms were full with stones—they weren't big enough to be called rocks—she dropped them next to him. He was scraping at the dirt, making the hole deeper than she thought was possible with the ground still partially frozen. After throwing the tainted meat to the bottom of the hole, he scooped the stones on top. He then shoved the dirt back in place and pounded the ground hard, first with his fists, then with his feet.

Aileen hoped Rhys had indeed made it impossible for wolves—or any other four-legged creature—to get to the poison. Only when he finished and some of the tension drained out of him did she breathe easier.

"I'm so sorry," she said, connecting with him in a way she hadn't done before. "That was the last thing I expected to see. I was hoping *not* to find such blatant hatred for wolves. If the traps were meant specifically for them."

"Believe me, they were. This is the heart of the pack's territory. A couple of big mouths have been bragging how they're going to rid the area of the wolf pack."

Did he mean Knute, the guy at the Cozy Café?

she wondered. Or were there a lot more antiwolf people around than she had counted on?

Whatever they thought, it was against the law for them to set traps for wolves. She could understand why an angry farmer or rancher who lost his stock to a wolf might grab his shotgun or rifle in retaliation—illegal as that might be.

As to the saw-toothed leghold traps, they harked back to the days of wolf extirpation in the early to mid-twentieth century. Unfortunately some trappers still used them. An animal caught in one of these would try to chew off its own leg to free itself. Thankfully, there had been no animal in that trap, but the thought of what might have been put a lump in Aileen's throat.

His anger spent, Rhys walked at a slower pace than previously when they set off again. Just as they crested a mound, he put out a hand to stay her and put a finger to his lips, then held two fingers over his head—which she took to mean he was making ears, as in those of a wolf.

Slowly advancing downhill toward the creek, he indicated she should follow.

Aileen swallowed hard and tried to breathe normally, difficult at best when she was so suddenly charged up. The staff came in handy now. Rhys seemed to be focused on something in the distance. Her gaze followed his. When she saw his target, her breath caught in her throat and she tripped over her own snowshoes. Luckily she had the staff to catch herself.

And then she took a better look at the magnificent timber wolf who seemed to be staring straight at her. Her head began to swim and her heart smacked up against her ribs, and she hung tightly onto her staff.

The wolf sniffed the air and backed up a few steps.

Rhys crouched and howled softly, raising the flesh along her spine.

The wolf looked from the wolf man to her as if trying to make up its mind.

It was afraid of her, Aileen thought. "Back at you," she whispered.

She'd been both looking forward to and dreading this moment for years. Face-to-face with a wolf in the wild! Exhilaration filled her and she stood her ground, took in every detail that she could.

The wolf looked something like a rangy husky with matted fur, long skinny legs and a bushy tail nearly a third the length of its body. From its size— maybe a hundred pounds or so—she figured this was a male. The long coarse guard hairs of his coat were mostly gray with some white mixed in. Though she was too far away to see them to be sure, his eyes undoubtedly were a pale brown or yellow.

Those eyes were glued to her, and Aileen wondered if the wolf was sizing her up the way she was him. Then, seeming startled, the wolf looked away first, pointy nose suddenly sniffing in a different direction.

Just as a shot shattered the forest silence...

Chapter Five

Acting on pure instinct, Rhys tackled Aileen and sent her flying to the earth even as second and third shots rang out, scattering the snow around them. He lay over her, his body shielding hers from the hunter. Faolan was safe, had taken off. Rhys barely got a glimpse of his bushy tail as it disappeared through the trees. The hunter would never get the wolf now. But he was still out there, armed and dangerous, and beneath him, Aileen trembled.

"You're shooting at people!" he yelled, willing to do what was necessary to protect them both. "And you'd better get out of here before I shoot back!"

Aileen's terror pulsed at him, but she didn't say a word. She was gasping as if trying to catch her breath.

"I'll protect you," he promised.

At least he hoped he could. He could guarantee nothing, not in this climate of fear created by deaths he didn't want to examine too closely.

Another shot rang out, closer this time—and after he'd shouted the warning. Rhys's muscles bunched up as he realized the wolf might not have been the intended target. When a second shot whizzed over their heads, he was certain of it.

"What are we going to do?" Aileen whispered.

"Stay calm."

One minute went by. Then another. No more shots.

Rhys cocked his head and listened. A faint sound pinpointed the enemy withdrawing. He was already too far away to give Rhys any idea of who was out there.

Getting to his feet and taking his rifle, he said, "Stay put and stay down!" Then he set off to follow without looking back to see if Aileen had obeyed.

Not that he could go as fast as he might like in the damn snowshoes. Not that he knew exactly what he was going to do when he caught up to the bastard. Concentrating his senses, he moved faster than a normal man even as he picked up sounds ahead. The chase was on. The bastard was running.

Even so, Rhys caught sight of a couple of footprints before they disappeared altogether in a rocky, sunlit area where the snow had melted. Recognizing the circle and wave pattern, he tugged off his snowshoes while still moving. Up he went, rifle still in hand, straight to the top of the rocky rise. Then he stopped and concentrated his senses in hopes of figuring out the direction the other man had taken.

A flick of movement between trees below caught his eye, but he quickly spotted a raccoon foraging for food. A sound to the east proved to be a rabbit hopping through snow. He raised his face to the west and breathed in, but the only scent that filled him was that of deer. And another wolf.

He'd lost the bastard! Damn it all!

Growling his displeasure, Rhys gripped his rifle hard and turned back in the direction from which he'd come. He was halfway down the incline when he spotted it.

The hunter's rifle—it had to be.

He picked it up. The barrel was still warm. He looked around again. How the hell had the owner disappeared so completely?

Taking the hunter's rifle with him, Rhys headed back the way he'd come, stopping only long enough to retrieve his snowshoes and put them back on before rejoining Aileen, who despite his warning, had gotten off the ground.

"Rhys, was someone really shooting at us?"

She was staring at the two rifles in his hands.

"A warning," he said. One that—if not heeded—could turn to something deadly.

"Warning?"

Caught by Aileen's tone, he looked down at her, but didn't answer because he didn't have one. He'd never faced anything like this before.

"I'm not sure what's going on here. Maybe it's part of the hysteria created by Patterson's death. Someone unstable is willing to take out his fear on humans who support the wolves as well as on the wolves themselves."

And then there was the footprint—he wondered what to make of that.

"The second rifle," Aileen said, interrupting his thoughts. "How did you get it?"

"The hunter must've dropped it." Or tossed it, though he didn't know why.

"Maybe the authorities can trace it back to the owner."

"If it was properly registered," he agreed.

"What about the wolf?" she asked.

"Gone." So she wouldn't misunderstand, he added, "Faolan got away safe."

"The wolves have names?"

"Why not?"

He caught her gaze and she didn't look away and she didn't shut him out. Fright had made her vulnerable—for the first time he was able to read her.

Pure emotion poured from her and he had that nagging sense of knowing her again.

But how could that be? Surely he would remember her if they'd met before. Her face, her form—they were somehow familiar and yet not. The only thing he recognized for certain was her scent. And the emotion that battered him in waves, that filled him with a wanting he couldn't express. He'd never experienced anything like it. Except once, long ago…

He peered deep into her and what he saw there disturbed him. Beyond her softness, beyond her kind nature, he saw something dark. A shadow that colored everything she did. That preyed upon her mind and on her heart. Something had robbed her of her innocence.

He blinked and the pathway instantly shuttered.

Rhys had never felt so alive…had never wanted anything so much as he did this woman. An impossible situation.

"Not exactly the introduction to your wolf pack that I'd hoped for," Aileen muttered.

Rhys stepped closer and brushed some snow off the back of her jacket. Suddenly he realized fear radiated from Aileen once more, but this was a fear different from that for the hunter. It went deeper and it was for him.

Though he wanted to reassure Aileen that she had no reason to fear him, he said nothing.

Lying wasn't in his nature.

JENS WAS NOWHERE TO BE SEEN when they got back to the cabin, and one of the snowmobiles was gone. And when Rhys put his rifle back on the rack, Aileen realized the other rack was empty. Good. After what she'd just been through, she didn't need Jens giving her any more of his disapproving expressions. She just wanted to freshen up and get back to the lodge. She'd had enough for one day. Enough for her whole stay. Unfortunately, her time here wasn't looking as idyllic as it had when she'd decided to make the trip.

"Relax by the fire and I'll make you some tea," Rhys suggested.

He'd convinced her to unwind before heading back to the lodge. But now that she was here, she couldn't seem to relax. She paced in front of the fireplace while he set a kettle on the stove. The main room of the cabin was an open area combining living room and dining room and kitchen.

"Are you going to report the hunter?" she asked.

"Of course I'll inform Randy Caine, for all the good it will do."

"You don't think Sheriff Caine will take you seriously?" She remembered him winking conspiratorially at Knute in the café. Still…"The hunter shot at *us*."

"They'll believe me, but no one was hurt, not

even a wolf. I don't expect they're going to put a team of experts on the case so they could give the bastard a warning when they track him down. Assuming they could do so from the serial number."

Something told her that Rhys could track him down. And considering how angry he'd been, he just might. A thought that made Aileen edgy again. Moving around the room and noting a small grouping of photographs of a teenaged Rhys, some with Jens, she asked, "How pervasive is the antiwolf sentiment in this area?"

"Not very. At least it wasn't. But there are always a few idiots. And with the recent suspicious deaths, fear is spreading."

"Deaths? As in plural?" This was the first she'd heard of it.

"Two before Patterson—one last fall, a second a few months back. All found in the woods. All autopsied."

"Why suspicious, then?"

"They weren't found immediately after death."

Which meant wild animals had probed at them, also, like Tom Patterson.

"The wolf haters aren't the only problem," he went on. "The DNR has talked about capturing a few wolves to test them for rabies or some other disease that would explain why they might attack humans."

"But I thought the autopsies proved wolves didn't kill anyone."

"The bodies have all been found in forested areas. So they're under pressure to come up with answers."

If that were true, quarantining the captured animals for ten days to see if rabies developed might very well be out of the question. The only other way to determine if a wolf had rabies was to cut off its head and test the brain for the virus.

"Tea will be ready in a minute," Rhys said.

Unsettled by the newest information, Aileen wandered into the library, once more amazed by the number of books. The one Rhys had been reading caught her eye. She'd meant to get a look at it, to see if it could give her new information for her thesis. Picking it up, she glanced at the title. *Werewolf: Myth or Reality?*

Her fingers suddenly numb, Aileen dropped the book back on the table.

"Hey, here's your tea."

She whipped around to face Rhys, wanting to ask him about the book. What was all this interest in werewolves? First Madam Sofia, now Rhys. But she couldn't form the question. It was too ridiculous.

"You know, it's later than I thought. I really need to get back to the lodge."

"I can take you. The snowmobile will fit in the back of my truck."

She ignored the offer and danced around him out of the room. "Listen, thanks for today, even if—"

"Aileen, wait."

But suddenly driven to leave, to get somewhere she could feel safe, she was already across the room. She unhooked her jacket from the peg by the door, which she opened before getting dressed. Rhys was standing in the library doorway, a mug in each hand and wearing a perplexed expression.

"Thanks, again," she called before whipping out of the cabin.

Unable to get to her snowmobile fast enough, she drove away from the cabin without a backward glance, but as she went up the incline, she swore she felt Rhys's eyes on her. Was he really standing at a window, staring after her or not? She refused to look back to find out.

All the way back to the lodge, she tried to make plans. What next? Who to interview? What Web sites to look up?

But even though she was determined not to think about anything negative, thoughts of men hunting wolves and werewolves hunting men filled her mind.

Not that she believed in werewolves!

But how could she not be spooked after the day she'd had? Her nerves were justified. Had those shots been warnings meant to drive her off because she'd been asking too many questions? What if she didn't go, what then? She couldn't think like that, not if she wanted to finish what she'd come for. That someone was trying to scare her put her back up. An angry McKenna stood her ground.

Even so, the lodge coming into view was a relief. The light was fading fast, but at least she'd gotten back before dark. She turned the snowmobile toward the open area in front of the shed, in time to see Fisk talking to another man. It was the guy from the café—Knute.

Slowing the snowmobile to a crawl, she wondered if something was going on. They were huddled together, expressions intense. Fisk seemed put out about something. And then they seemed to realize they weren't alone and broke apart.

Knute took one look at her as she parked the snowmobile and asked, "Enjoy your excursion into *wolf* territory?"

Aileen's heart skipped a beat. Had he been the one to shoot at her and Rhys? "Enjoy hunting today?"

"I woulda enjoyed it more if I'd a gotten what I went out for."

"Sometimes the prey turns on the hunter," she said, her pulse jagging as she baited him. She couldn't help herself. She was still angry. "You ought to be careful."

Scowling, he stalked away, head down, jamming fists into his pockets and muttering to himself. Aileen swore she heard him say something about wolf lovers needing a lesson. From him?

"Didn't expect you back so soon," Fisk said matter-of-factly.

She parked the snowmobile and got off. "Yeah, things didn't work out the way I thought they would."

"That happens."

"Sorry to interrupt you. I seem to have scared away your company."

"Knute? He's not company. He's my little brother. And his leaving had nothing to do with you."

Though Aileen wasn't certain of that, she chose not to argue the point.

"By the way," Fisk said, "I got to that mess on your deck. I replaced the trim. Paint might still be wet, so be careful if you go out there."

"Uh, thanks."

She started off for the lodge, her steps reluctant.

Safe... She'd wanted to go someplace safe. Instead she was going to a room where something had tried to get to her the night before.

She stopped and stared up at the deck and considered the impossibility of getting up there without a ladder or the ability to climb a tree.

She turned back and saw that the handyman was checking over the snowmobile she'd borrowed. "Say, Fisk?"

"Something I can do for you?"

"Any idea of how that wood got torn up?"

"Some guest had a dog and put it out there," Fisk said.

He didn't sound like he believed that story any more than she did. But what other explanation was there?

And thinking it was anything else was simply crazy.

Still, she had to ask, "Wolves don't come in this close to town, do they?"

"Wolves?" Fisk's tone changed. Darkened. "Better not. After what's been going on around here, a wolf would be shot, sure enough."

Would he do the shooting himself? Aileen wondered, now suspicious of everyone. She hated thinking Fisk could be so despicable as to shoot at her. Or at the wolves. Bad enough his brother Knute was out to get them.

Swallowing hard, she croaked out a "Thanks" before heading for the lodge and dinner. Despite her sudden lack of appetite, her stomach was grumbling.

Maybe cougars were around in addition to the wolves and Valerie didn't want to scare off her guests by saying so. That was probably it, she thought. Some big cat had climbed the tree and had tried to get in. That had to be it.

So why didn't she believe that, either? Aileen wondered.

She didn't stop until she got to the front door. And then, before opening it and going inside the lodge, she looked behind her into the deepening gloom.

And up above the line of trees, the waxing moon...

AGITATED, TRYING TO RUN off his dismal mood, Rhys returned to the cabin as darkness spread over the forest. He sprinted for the front door just as it opened. Father was fully dressed and about to leave.

"About time you got back."

Chest heaving for air, Rhys said, "But I made it. Father, you know what I want."

The old man's features tightened. "Don't be ridiculous. You have nothing to fear."

"We don't know that."

Rhys glanced up to the darkening sky and saw the shadow of the moon that would be full in a few days. "I know it. I know you. Besides, you have protection. It's not necessary."

"But it's what I want. Please."

"It's not right. No, I won't do it."

His father pushed by him and Rhys looked after him feeling helpless. "Please, you have to lock me up so I can't get out tonight!"

But head down, mumbling to himself, the man who'd saved his life ignored him and kept going.

Leaving Rhys with a sense of doom he couldn't shake.

THE HUNTER ZIGZAGGED through the pines, focused on the night's prey. The bloodlust had been growing and multiplying. Tonight, the hunger had become intolerable.

At the edge of the woods, the hunter stopped and peered into the clearing. The lodge rose into the night. The windows shone and were shadowed by occasional movement. Music pulsed from the downstairs, and even at this distance, the loud throbbing hurt.

Closer, another building. Movement there, too.

The hunter hunkered to the ground and waited and hungered.

The hour grew late. The lights in the lodge windows dimmed. The music stopped.

And then the prey stepped into the clearing, bright hair lit by moonlight.

Now...

Coming closer, the prey seemed oblivious to any danger.

The hunter coiled, ready to spring.

Wait a while longer. The prey entered the woods. Better that the kill was away from the lodge, away from those who would seek retribution.

The hunter followed behind for a distance—far enough that they entered a part of the forest rarely traversed by people. Moving parallel with the prey brought sweet music to the hunter's ears.

Heart pounding...breathing ragged...footsteps speeding up...

The hunter sped up, too, allowing a single rumble as warning. The prey glanced back, face suddenly contorted by fear as the hunter pounced. Flesh tore and bone broke and the hunter became lost in the bloodlust.

Chapter Six

Ow-ow-owooooo...

The howl thrills her all the way to her bare toes as she wanders away from the campsite.

The fog is thick, the forest floor covered with the rot of decay. She glances back at the tent where Dad and Skelly and Donovan sleep. How many times had they been told never to leave the tent alone at night, not even to go to the bathroom?

Another howl dispels her uncertainty.

Every night, the wolf's lonely cries call to her, fill her with longing.

Ow-ow-owooooo...ow-ow-owooooo...

Aileen awoke with a start, the wolf's howls haunting her once again.

It was morning, shafts of gray light spilling into the room. That last dream had been so real...almost like a memory.

Could it be?

Aileen shivered. The area had some hold on her, but try as she had, she'd never remembered anything that had happened on that night all those years ago.

Could being here now bring back whatever it was that had happened to her?

Glancing at the clock, she realized she'd over-slept and immediately climbed out of bed. Ana-lyzing the past could wait until later.

No sun to wipe away the restless night that had been filled with wild dreams about wolves and hunters. Having awakened countless times with her heart pounding, her adrenaline buzzing through her, Aileen was happy that she would be spending a quiet few hours in the company of loved ones.

After a quick shower, she threw on her clothes and rushed through the lodge, arriving in sync with her brother. His black truck was just stopping at the front door.

Her face set in a scowl, Valerie was on a ladder, messing with a light fixture. Surprised, Aileen wondered why Fisk wasn't doing the job.

"Morning, Valerie."

The owner started, then seemed to realize she was going out. "You have plans for the day?"

"Family plans."

"If you need equipment for later, tell me now and I'll set it out for you. I might not be around."

Undoubtedly, Sunday was Fisk's day off, leaving Valerie to take care of his duties. "That would be great. Snowshoes and a snowmobile would do it."

"No problem," Valerie muttered, getting back to her task.

Aileen slipped out into the cold. Donovan was out of the truck and opening the door for her. Realizing he was alone, she asked, "Are we meeting Laurel and the baby in town at the café?"

"Who said anything about a café? We're having brunch at home."

When he climbed behind the wheel, she said, "I didn't mean for you to go to all that trouble!"

"You're no trouble. You're my sister. And we needed to eat with or without you. I'm pleased it's with."

"If I know Laurel, she's killing herself to make a feast."

"How do you know *I'm* not the one cooking?"

"Moose stew for brunch?"

Donovan grinned. "Snake omelet."

"The snakes haven't roused themselves from their winter sleep yet."

"Could have had some in the freezer."

Aileen stared at her brother's profile. "You're a changed man. You joke and everything. Laurel has got to be the best thing that's ever happened to you."

"And our daughter."

"And Willow," Aileen agreed, looking forward to her first peek at the newest McKenna.

"I take it you've settled in okay."

"Like I told you, the lodge is very comfortable."

"That's not what I mean. I'm more interested in your comfort zone in the area…in the forest and all."

Aileen knew he was referring to the past. "I'm all grown up, Donovan. I can handle anything." Even bizarre dreams that felt like bits of memory.

"I believe you can."

"I am a McKenna, after all."

Donovan grinned and Aileen settled down inside.

A quarter of an hour later, just as she spotted a sign that indicated Iron Lake was ahead, he turned the truck onto a side road that headed first across fields that belonged to farms, but eventually led into the woods. A mile or so later, he turned onto an even smaller, curvy road lined with conifers. Suddenly a house appeared in a clearing. Rather a giant log cabin with a windowed wall overlooking the small lake that was part of Donovan's property.

The moment the truck stopped, Aileen scrambled out and headed for the front door that held one of the biggest Christmas wreaths she'd ever seen. Then the door opened to reveal a grinning Laurel. The women hugged and Aileen stepped into the huge great room with floor-to-ceiling knotty pine, a stone fireplace and a large loft. Everything was decorated for the holiday and the air was filled with cinnamon.

Glancing beneath the tree, Aileen said, "Wow, those are some presents."

"For lots and lots of McKennas," Laurel said, reminding her of the family holiday gathering to be held here. "Mere days until they start descending on us."

Aileen's stomach growled at the wonderful food smells filling the house but she ignored her hunger, asking, "So, where is my new niece?"

"Right this way," Laurel said, heading into the kitchen area.

Willow was asleep in what looked to be a handmade cradle. Aileen stared down at the chubby, dark-haired baby and couldn't stop the smile that attacked her lips. "She's beautiful."

"We think so," Laurel said in a low voice. "Now how about that breakfast?"

Aileen felt a flutter in her chest. Would she ever have a child of her own? Her biological clock was ticking and she wasn't even dating anyone at the moment. At least she would have Willow as her godchild, a little girl to spoil.

"I'm starving," she agreed, reluctantly backing away from the cradle. "Let's eat."

Laurel had indeed created a feast. A homemade coffee cake, a frittata and thick slices of bacon washed down with fresh orange juice and French Roast coffee.

As they ate, Aileen brought them up to date on the Chicago branch of the McKenna family. Then, knowing her sister-in-law came from Chicago, as well, she asked, "How about you, Laurel? Do you ever miss living in the big city?"

"Sometimes, but I've really grown to love it out here."

Laurel was looking at Donovan in a way that made Aileen realize her sister-in-law would love it anywhere she could be with him. Her throat tightened. None of her relationships had lasted for more than a few months—probably because they hadn't been the happily ever after sort.

Oddly, Rhys's penetrating gaze came to mind…

"You're not worried about moving to a rural area, are you?" Laurel asked, interrupting the unwelcome thought. "You don't really have to live in the forest to work in your field."

"Uh, no." Flustered that she'd been thinking about the wolf man, Aileen pulled herself back together. "Not unless I want to. And on my days off I can always head out for Chicago and stay with Dad or Skelly." The *forest* reference still being a source of unease and probably would remain so until she sorted out the past.

"So tell us about yesterday," Donovan said. "Did Lindgren show you his wolves?"

Uh-oh. "One wolf. Just one." Uncomfortable after thinking about Rhys and relationships in the same mind frame, Aileen quickly turned the questioning around. "So I hear there were a couple of other mysterious outdoor deaths this year, one of them just a few months ago."

"Wolves didn't kill them, either."

"It just looked like they did," Laurel added.

"To *some* people." Donovan scowled. "One man fell and split his head open on a rock. The other drowned in a lake not too far from here."

"I thought they were both partially eaten," Aileen said.

"They were. The body apparently washed up on shore before he became some animal's dinner."

A heart attack…a head split open…a drowning…and all three had become food for nature. How common was that? Aileen wondered. Not very, not to her knowledge.

"So tell us more about your adventure with Rhys Lindgren," Donovan said just as the baby began to wail.

"My niece is awake!" Aileen popped out of her chair before Laurel could. "I'll get her."

Grateful for the reprieve, Aileen picked up a wailing Willow and made soothing sounds as she cuddled the baby to her. She didn't dare tell her brother about being shot at or he might try to interfere, try to keep her from going out into the field with Rhys again.

Nothing was going to stop her now.

AILEEN FIGURED ON TAKING it easy when she got back to the lodge. She could curl up by the fireplace downstairs to work on her thesis, maybe nap a little later. For a couple of hours, she followed that plan, modifying her thesis outline and searching the Internet for information. She found a couple of personal stories of wolf encounters, but nothing that came close to what Rhys had described to her.

Rhys…why couldn't she stop thinking about him? He'd been in her dreams, too, along with wolves. And the more she thought about him, the more she wanted to see him. Rather the more she wanted to see his interaction with his wolves, Aileen told herself. Her interest was strictly professional.

His wolves…of course they weren't *his*…the pack had simply made the Lindgren homestead part of their territory. A territory that had turned dangerous.

Had Rhys gotten the rifle to the authorities, and if so, what had been the result?

A vehicle pulling in made her look out the window. Valerie exited a red SUV in a hurry. Then she hesitated, hefted the keys in her hand, opened the door and stuck the keys between the sunshade and roof.

An action that would be chancy in the big city, Aileen thought. But she knew lots of people who lived in the country did that. Obviously there was a trust factor here that she couldn't comprehend.

Valerie whipped into the lodge and went directly into her office without so much as acknowledging Aileen's presence. Obviously, she was still in a mood.

Aileen worked a bit longer and then grabbed a late lunch. She gave up the nap idea. Unable to wait any longer to find out what happened with the rifle, she called Rhys.

"Lindgren residence," Jens answered.

"Rhys, please."

"Who is this?"

"Aileen McKenna."

"Rhys isn't here!" His tone was clipped.

"Can you tell me when he'll be back?"

"This isn't a good time. Leave well enough alone!"

With that, Jens slammed the phone down at his

end. At first Aileen was shocked by the man's rudeness and simply stared at the telephone for a moment. Then she calmed down and dressed for the outdoors.

Once outside, she grabbed the snowshoes Valerie had set out for her. She lashed them to the back of a snowmobile, after which she set off for the heart of wolf territory. Undoubtedly, Rhys couldn't come to the phone because he wasn't home—he must be out there himself.

Avoiding the Lindgren cabin, Aileen continued on the snowmobile toward the area they'd covered the day before. Remembering Rhys's warning about the noise scaring away the pack, she went as far as she dared before abandoning the snowmobile. Then she affixed the snowshoes to her boots, and after looking around carefully to make sure nothing set the hair at the back of her neck to attention, she set off on foot.

Keeping her senses attuned to her surroundings—not wanting any more unpleasant surprises—she retraced the route she'd taken with Rhys. Past the campfire. Past the spot where he'd found the leghold trap. Her heart beat a little faster and she was having some trouble breathing, so she stopped for a moment and checked out the area again.

Going on, just before reaching the incline

leading down to the creek, she heard a yip. The tempo of her heartbeat shifted into high gear as she strained to hear more.

"You like that, do you?"

The faint words drifted over the ridge to her. Rhys. As did the animal sounds in response. Her mouth went dry. It sounded like Rhys was communicating with the wild wolf pack.

The thought that she was really so close to them paralyzed her for a moment. She forced herself to move—she had to see the wild wolf-human interaction for herself.

Cresting the rise, she stopped again, pulse pounding. As if he sensed her there, Rhys looked straight at her a millisecond before the wolves did the same. Coincidence, she thought, knowing human senses weren't nearly as developed as those of animals.

There were five wolves surrounding Rhys— three adults and two juveniles—their fur going from brown to gray to black. They backed away but didn't run. Instead, they all swung spooked gazes from her to him, as if ready to take their cue from Rhys's reaction to her.

Though his visage darkened as if he was displeased to see her, he hunkered down on a fallen log next to the creek's edge and she heard him murmur, "Relax, Aileen's a friend."

He touched the wolf closest to him—one of the juveniles—and the animal huddled against his leg.

Like a dog, Aileen thought. The wolf was acting like one of its domesticated canine cousins. She'd jokingly thought of Rhys as the wolf man before, but now it seemed the nickname really fit him.

Not knowing what else to do—she didn't want to scare them away—Aileen held her ground and silently observed as Rhys continued to glare at her while talking to the wolves in a soft, persuasive voice. One by one, they seemed to relax and went about their business—drinking water from the creek, marking territory and, in the case of the juveniles, finding a rock and playing canine soccer with it.

Aileen was stunned and moved, and as she watched, she felt herself relax a little, as well. What had she expected them to do? Attack her?

Now why would she think that? What would make that thought even enter her head?

Maybe three men in a year who'd fallen prey to something with sharp teeth…

Rhys was the only one paying her any mind. He was the only one who seemed to be perturbed by her presence. He rose from the log and slowly eased his way over to where she still stood. His expression was as dark as a thundercloud. Her heart thudded and her mouth went dry, but she met him halfway down the incline.

"What the hell are you doing here?" he demanded, keeping his tone low and even.

"Isn't it obvious?"

"You must have a very short memory."

Though she knew it was a reference to the hunter, she said, "I didn't get to see this."

He glowered at her, saying, "You need to leave. The woods are dangerous at dark."

And though she felt ready to jump out of her skin, she held her ground. "It's not even dusk yet."

"Aileen, go! Now!"

They were glaring at each other, both frozen to the spot. Aileen couldn't believe Rhys was being so high-handed. Just like Jens. He might not look like his father, but he certainly had the man's temperament.

A splash drew her attention back to the pack, and she realized the wolves were all staring at the humans—no doubt alarmed by the altercation.

Before she could back down, Rhys grabbed her arm, saying, "If you won't go yourself—"

Suddenly he stopped as if interrupted and whipped around. Aileen followed his gaze. There on the other side of the creek stood a large gray wolf, the edges of its mouth curled into a snarl. Her insides lurched and Rhys let her go and made his way back down to the creek.

"Rhys, what are you doing?"

He didn't answer and she tried not to panic.

This wolf looked dangerous and big enough to take down a man…exactly what the lone wolf seemed intent on doing. No doubt he was a disperser, looking for a pack to rule by challenging the alpha male and driving him away. He looked from Rhys to the brown male, undoubtedly the leader of the pack.

But when the gray lunged, it was at Rhys.

Aileen gasped in horror. Thoughts of Tom Patterson and the other deaths suddenly jarring her, she immediately looked for some weapon—a rock or a limb she could use to drive away the animal—but Rhys reacted faster.

He grabbed onto the gray and threw him down into the creek, holding him in the water for several seconds to subdue him, as if letting him know who was boss. Power seemed to emanate off him and Aileen had a sense of déjà vu. Ridiculous, of course, for she'd never seen human-wolf interaction. When Rhys let go, the wolf scrambled to his feet and shot off through the trees, his tail between his legs.

The wolves whined and crowded around Rhys.

Unnerved, Aileen stared at him, wondering what it was she had just witnessed. He'd subdued the animal without hurting him, as if claiming his dominance.

As if *he* were the alpha male.

Her blood felt as if it were racing through her at accelerated speed. Her head went light as if it wanted to take her someplace she was reluctant to go. She fought the sensation, but then Rhys caught her gaze and it intensified.

He patted the closest wolves and moved toward her, his power washing over her as it had the challenger.

"Wh-what happened?" she gasped as he walked right through her defenses and pulled her into his arms as if trying to subdue *her*.

Or at least calm her.

He had the opposite effect. Something was happening to her that she didn't understand. When he looked deep into her eyes, she felt him inside her again, but this time she couldn't fight it—couldn't fight him. Couldn't fight the kiss that seemed as natural as anything she'd witnessed here.

When his lips crushed hers, Aileen threw her arms around his neck and her body against his and kissed him back as if it would relieve this fever that had suddenly gripped her. She met him with the same fierceness he possessed. She was drowning in emotion. In sensations. Both accelerated, threatening to take her to a place she wasn't willing to go.

Fear drove her out of his arms.

And like the gray wolf, she ran away, tail between her legs, as fast as she could go.

He'd been serious when he said the woods were dangerous.

Too bad the danger was Rhys himself.

SOMETIME LATER, AILEEN stopped to catch her breath and get her bearings. Panic had made her careless. Either she'd run in the wrong direction or she'd passed the snowmobile without ever seeing it.

Being lost deep in the forest alone wasn't reassuring. Her skin crawled and stomach spiraled. Remnants of the dreams came back to her. She wanted out and she wanted out now. Turning in a circle, she looked for something familiar but it all looked the same to her. In every direction, trees and shadows mocked her. She had the sense that something was very wrong…and very familiar.

The dream had to be what was spooking her. *Settle down,* she told herself. *Think.*

Of course, the thing to do would be to follow her own snowshoe tracks back the way she had come. Even so, she hesitated. In that path lay the real danger of the forest. A real live wolf man. Only why had she been so spooked by a kiss?

Gathering her inner resources, she set out on her way, determined to face him if she must, unable to stop thinking about what she'd felt. What she'd seen.

It hadn't been the kiss itself that had frightened her. It had been the way Rhys had handled the disperser wolf. The way the other wolves had been subservient to him. The way she'd responded as if she had no mind of her own.

Aileen was so wrapped up in her thoughts that once again she found herself veering off in the wrong direction. She stood in the middle of an unfamiliar clearing. Frustrated, she started to turn back, to pick up her prints, when her attention zeroed in on splashes of darkening red against the melting snow.

Barely breathing, she stood frozen, unable to move anything but her eyes. She swept her gaze along the trail of red to a log at the edge of the clearing. Something stuck out awkwardly from behind it.

A booted foot.

"God, no…"

Though repelled at what she knew she would find, Aileen couldn't stop herself from moving forward. Her heart bumped against her ribs and

her pulse jagged along her veins. She had to see...
had to...

Keeping the log between her and the body as
if it would protect her, she leaned forward. The
far arm came into view. No hand. Cloth shredded.
Shoulder a mass of torn flesh and jagged bone.
But it was the face—what was left of the face—
that paralyzed her.

For a moment she lost her voice.

And then she screamed.

Chapter Seven

The scream raised the fine hairs on the back of his neck and—having no doubt that Aileen was in trouble—Rhys was off like a shot after her.

The wolves scattered and as he drove through the trees, birds fluttered up, their wings flapping as fast as his accelerated heartbeat.

"Ai-le-e-en!" he yelled, but nothing more than the sound of his own jagged breath filled his head. What if she were hurt? She couldn't be. But if she was, he had to find her and fast! He picked up his pace and slowed his breathing, and a moment later—intently focusing all his senses—tried again. "Aileen! Where are you?"

"Over here!" Her muted cry came from the west.

Immediately relieved that she was able to answer him, Rhys yelled, "I'm coming! Stay put!" and shifted direction, heading straight for her, quickly fine-tuning the faint sounds warring with one another.

The sun was setting, streaks of bright light shooting through apertures in the forest, nearly blinding Rhys. He shadowed his eyes and pushed forward toward a clearing in the trees ahead. Able to sense Aileen now, he glanced up only to see her swaying over a sea of red.

His gut clenched… Stopping to catch his breath in relief, Rhys was instead left with a shaky gut and the realization that blood had indeed been spilled here.

Its metallic scent nearly strangled him.

Not Aileen's blood…

She was standing over something…someone…still quietly sniffling but in control. But the thing on the ground…*the person*…he shook his head and, in a daze, stepped toward her.

Just then, she turned to face him. "Oh, Rhys, thank God," she whispered, moving away from the dark blot in the snow toward him.

Rhys thought he was going to be sick. Father hadn't locked him up the night before.

What if…

Aileen threw herself into his arms. Rhys clasped her to him, smoothed her back through her parka and peered over her shoulder at what he could see of the remains of a man who'd been ripped apart.

"He's d-dead…l-like the others…" Her voice

trembled as deeply as did her body. "….only he h-hasn't been out here long."

The scent was strong enough to indicate a fresh kill. Remembering the full moon last night, Rhys asked, "How can you be sure?"

"Because yesterday he was alive!"

Last night had been the last time he'd seen Father. His throat went tight and Rhys forced out a single word.

"Who?"

Aileen sniffed and said, "Valerie's handyman—Fisk Oeland."

Rhys's knees went weak. It wasn't relief he felt. How could it be? That Jens Lindgren was alive didn't absolve him of the sick feeling in his gut.

He couldn't remember anything that happened last night, not between his argument with Father and waking up with the wolves that morning.

Just as it happened so many times before.

And now…another man was dead.

AUTHORITIES SWARMED THE death site. The sheriff. A couple of deputies. The coroner and his team. And a wildlife expert from the DNR. Rhys was talking to him now, but Aileen wished he were here at her side. Sheriff Caine was on the offensive and Aileen was getting more nervous by the minute.

"So you just happened to stumble across the

body," Sheriff Caine commented, scribbling something into his notebook.

"Not stumbled exactly—"

Caine fixed her with that spooky gray gaze of his. "But that's what you said."

"I wasn't being literal. I lost my snowmobile and was looking for it and I saw something—"

"The body?"

"A foot and—"

"Why were you wandering around these parts, anyway?" he demanded.

"I came out to look for Rhys—"

"So you didn't find him? He found you?"

"Yes. I mean, no. I found him but—"

"Then why weren't you with him?"

"If you would ever let me finish a sentence," Aileen said in exasperation, "I could tell you."

Caine stepped closer, making the flesh along Aileen's spine crawl. There was something about him…

"Look, miss," he said, his tone low and fake sweet, "you'd better cooperate here or I'll bring you in for questioning in Fisk's murder."

"That's enough!"

The bark came from Rhys, who moved from the DNR representative to stand protectively by Aileen's side. He was almost touching her—not quite—and she felt an immediate calm wash through her.

"Don't poke your nose where it don't belong, nature boy," Caine said.

"I wouldn't dream of it." Rhys drew Caine's gaze to him, where he caught and held it. "But it does belong here. I'm the one who called you, remember."

A staring contest. Aileen couldn't believe it. Like they were measuring each other up for some kind of pissing contest. Tension wired between the men. As strong as Caine was, Rhys was stronger. To her relief, his animal power made the sheriff look away first.

"All right. All right. I guess you did call me."

His questioning took on a more reasonable tone and Aileen answered what she could. All the while, she was aware of Rhys having her back. A good feeling.

"That's it, I guess. If I need more, I know where to find you."

Caine backed off and Rhys turned his attention to Aileen. "You all right?"

She nodded. "He just got me wired until you stepped in. Sheriff Caine doesn't like me."

"Don't take it personally. As far as I can tell, he doesn't much like anyone. Listen, I want to talk to the coroner for a minute. Will you be okay?"

Nodding, Aileen sat herself on a log stump a dozen yards away from the investigative activity. Her stomach felt like a lump of ice and the rest of her was quickly reaching that status. She could hear them discussing the situation, but the words jumbled in her head. Fisk Oeland was dead. A man she knew had been struck down by what appeared to be a wolf.

She could hardly believe it—not just that Fisk had been killed, but that a wolf was responsible. It went against everything that she'd thought she knew about the species. Then again, so had the earlier incident with the disperser wolf who'd attacked Rhys...

"Let's get you out of here," Rhys said some time later.

Still lost in thought, Aileen didn't respond until he hooked a hand under her arm and urged her to her feet. She rose and stared at him for a moment before blinking away the inertia and realizing he seemed concerned about her.

"I'm all right," she said. "Just thinking. A little out of focus."

"I expect so." His voice was tight, as was his body when he led her away from the death scene. "Sheriff Caine says he may follow up later. He knows where to find you."

Aileen glanced back, but when she saw the

coroner's men bag Fisk Oeland's body, she tore her gaze away.

"I don't know what else I can tell Sheriff Caine." It wasn't like she'd seen the kill. And if the sheriff kept at her, would he somehow get her to tell him about the wolf attack on Rhys right before she found the body? "Are they sure Fisk was mauled by a wolf? Or even that he wasn't already injured or dead before the animal got to him?"

"They won't be sure of anything until the autopsy. Maybe not even then."

The way Rhys said the last statement made Aileen frown. "They can tell whether or not the saliva came from a wolf?" It was possible that a feral dog could do the same damage—the saliva could be the key to determining the nature of the predator.

"That they can."

Rhys still sounded doubtful. He didn't seem in the mood to talk, though. His features looked to be set in stone and his mouth was drawn into a thin, hard line. Because of what had happened earlier? Whatever, Aileen sensed he was taking this personally and that it would be best if she kept her thoughts to herself for the moment. Though those thoughts raced through her mind like a rabbit heading for cover, she didn't say another word until they found her snowmobile right where she'd left it.

"Do you want me to come back to the cabin with you?" she asked as she climbed on.

"I'm not going home just yet. Don't worry, I'll see you back to the lodge."

"I can get there on my own."

"You've had a terrible experience."

"I'm fine." As fine as she could be considering the circumstances. Embarrassed at how she'd broken down earlier, she tried to convince him with a calm expression and rueful smile. "Really."

Rhys frowned, then as if he believed her, he looked in the direction of the kill, making Aileen think he wanted to head right back there even though the body was probably already being hauled away.

She touched his arm. "The authorities have the situation in hand, Rhys."

"I'm not worried about the investigation. I need to know my wolves are all right."

His wolves. She'd chastised herself for thinking of them as such, but apparently he did, also.

She couldn't stop herself from asking, "What about the lone wolf that showed up this afternoon?"

"What about him?"

"Did he seem sick to you?"

"You think he's responsible?"

"I'm just asking."

"Be careful who you ask. Or who you tell

about what happened earlier," he went on, his voice getting strident. "That is, if you don't want a wolf kill on your conscience."

"Rhys!" She felt as if he'd just struck her. That would be the last thing she wanted.

Before she could reassure him, he said, "You know that's what'll happen if you tell anyone. The word will get around that there's a wolf stirring up trouble and the wolf haters will be in these woods by morning, guns loaded. They'll hunt him down and kill him. Rather any wolf they sight."

Having seen the results of this attack for herself, Aileen shifted uneasily. "But what if—"

"No! He's just looking for a pack."

Once again Rhys got to her and Aileen felt her temper rising. "A wolf who's trying to take over a pack would challenge the alpha male, not you."

She felt his gaze burn into her as he said, "I'm still alive, aren't I?"

"But Fisk Oeland isn't."

"That wolf didn't kill him!"

His response was so strident that Aileen could only gape at him for a moment. Finally, she regained her voice and forced herself to stay calm when she said, "You can't be certain of that."

Rhys shook his head and backed away. "I thought I knew you."

"It's not like I want it to be true."

But he kept going, turning and quickly melding with the shadows of the forest.

Leaving Aileen staring after him and wondering if Rhys knew something that he was keeping to himself.

As she headed for the lodge, a new dread filled her. Valerie. Would anyone have told the owner about Fisk's death yet? What if she ran into the other woman? Aileen certainly didn't want to be the bearer of that news. Bad enough she would have to call Donovan. For all she knew, her brother might already have heard about the death. And about the fact that she'd been the one to find the body.

Why her? she wondered.

Why did strange things happen to her in this area?

A flashback to that morning's dream made her shudder, and she forced herself to concentrate on the trail. She couldn't stop her mind from wandering to Rhys Lindgren, though, and wondering what he was doing now. His dedication to the wolves was so intense she wondered why he didn't formalize it by working for the DNR or heading one of the groups that supported wolf reintegration. Maybe it was the lack of a formal education that stopped him. Or maybe it was simply his personality. Taking matters into his own hands seemed to suit him.

Maybe like the male that had entered his pack's territory, Rhys was simply a lone wolf.

RHYS LOPED BACK TO THE kill site and stopped in a line of trees far enough back that he could see without being seen. Fisk Oeland's body had already been removed and everyone was gone but the sheriff and the coroner—both had lit-up cigarettes.

Though he remained where he was about a hundred feet away, his chest tight and gut knotted with tension, Rhys tuned in to their conversation.

"We're gonna have us a problem unless you can come up with some explanation that doesn't have to do with the wolves," Caine was saying.

"You want me to lie?"

"I want you to work extra hard to find extenuating circumstances for the folks in Wolf Creek."

"Huh, could've fooled me. I would've thought you'd want to get rid of the wolves."

Rhys started at the threat to the pack, but he kept himself from revealing himself.

"What I *don't* want," the sheriff said, "is a bunch of scared, angry people going off halfcocked into the woods with loaded guns. One of them could get shot, and a wolf kill would bring the feds down on us, for sure. Bad enough we have to deal with the DNR."

"I'll see what I can do," the coroner said. "If that's all?"

"Go."

Caine waved him off, but didn't immediately follow. The sheriff stood staring down at the bloodstained snow and finished his cigarette, then flicked away the butt. Finally he walked off through a stand of trees as an engine kicked to life. A moment later, Rhys heard a second engine and recognized it as belonging to the sheriff's four-wheel-drive SUV.

He stepped out into the clearing and approached the kill site. When he reached the log, he stooped to take a better look, something he hadn't been able to do earlier, not with all those people around.

Of course, now the site was disturbed. Lots of human footprints along with the animal's. A gray wolf's track was about four and a half inches long by three and a half inches wide. It fit. But that same print could have been made by a large dog or a hybrid wolf dog, the most dangerous animal of the three. Dangerous because hybrids were unpredictable. They seemed to be domesticated like dogs—they weren't afraid of human contact—but they still had the wild instincts of a wolf.

Rhys swept his gaze over the area, then stopped

and focused on a particular set of human prints. He drew closer to the circle and wave pattern that was becoming all too familiar. The same pattern he'd seen when chasing the hunter who'd taken those shots at him and Aileen. The same pattern he'd seen near Tom Patterson's body.

The prints were most vivid right where the coroner and sheriff had stood talking. A fact that gave him some personal measure of relief even as he realized what it might mean.

Before leaving the area, he found the cigarette butt flicked away by the sheriff and secured it in a small plastic bag from his pocket.

THE RESORT GROUNDS COMING into view were a welcome sight. Aileen maneuvered straight for the shed where she left the equipment before heading for the lodge.

Needing to call her brother and reassure him that she was all right, Aileen was doubly torn when she practically ran into Valerie upon entering the building. The owner was bundled up, obviously on her way out. From the other woman's distracted expression, Aileen gathered she didn't know about Fisk. And though it would be easier to leave it to someone else to give the owner the bad news, she simply couldn't.

"I need to talk to you for a moment, Valerie.

Something terrible has happened…out on the trail."

The skin between the owner's brows pulled and she looked out past Aileen as if she could see for herself. "What happened?"

"Another death…I found the body."

Valerie's eyes went wide. "Someone else is dead?"

Aileen nodded. "The authorities are out there now. It looked like he was attacked by a wild animal."

"A wolf attack?" Valerie sounded horrified.

She didn't want to say it—"Maybe…"—but that could be the truth.

As if she couldn't comprehend it, Valerie shook her head and her gaze seemed unfocused. "Who?"

Aileen took a deep breath. "Fisk. It was Fisk Oeland."

Valerie's eyes went wide. "Oh, no!"

"Maybe you should sit down."

Valerie was shaking her head and pushing toward the exit. "I need to get out there…see for myself." At the door, she paused and asked, "Where exactly did you find him?"

"It's been a while. The authorities will already have removed his body."

"Where?" Valerie asked again, her voice stronger this time.

Aileen gave her directions, ending with "You can probably follow my snowmobile tracks," but the lodge owner was already out the door and racing toward the equipment shed.

Figuring there wasn't anything she could do for the other woman, who seemed to be fired by a burst of adrenaline, Aileen went inside. A couple snuggling by the fire looked up for a second, then lost themselves in each other again.

Aileen headed for her room where she climbed onto the bed, pulled the quilt over her and put in that call to her brother. An uncomfortable conversation, but necessary. Thankfully Donovan didn't threaten to drag her away from Wolf Creek forcibly, though he was definitely concerned for her, as well as for the welfare of the wolves in the area. He made her promise to be careful, and in return he promised he would share any information he could from his end.

Not knowing what to do next, she waited.

Would Rhys call her and tell her everything was all right?

Was it?

Rhys hadn't been himself. Because he knew the wolf that had attacked him had killed Fisk?

Or because he knew something else, she wondered again, *something he wasn't telling...*

EERIE HOWLS FILL THE NIGHT, the midnight hour.

The wolf's mournful sound pulls her deeper and deeper into the woods and farther and farther from the family camp. The moon is full and fingers of pale light poke through the dense trees and ghostly fog. Her heart is beating so fast her chest hurts. She falls once, scraping her hand on a rock. It stings and it's bleeding, too, but she can't let it stop her.

Aileen's eyes flew open to a dark room.

How long had she been asleep?

Lulled by a past she couldn't resist, she closed her eyes and sought it…

She breaks through the stand and into a large clearing. There her wolf sits on a soft mound of flowered earth, its pointy nose raised as it sings a siren's song. Moonbeams gently limn its black fur with a silver-blue glow, and she stares, her mouth open. Though smaller than she'd expected—a young one?—she's thrilled.

This is the most beautiful creature she's ever seen.

"You don't have to be lonely anymore," she murmurs. "I'm here now."

A memory? Was it really a memory?

Would she finally be able to fill in the blank of her young life?

Aileen turned onto her side and brought the quilt with her and covered her head…

As if sensing her childlike admiration, the wolf

quiets and meets her gaze. The juvenile's pale amber eyes gleam and its tongue lolls from its mouth, making it look like a big, friendly dog. She holds out her hand and makes soft cooing sounds. Tail swishing, the wolf tentatively steps closer, as if wanting to trust her. Then its head whips up and it stops, body suddenly stiff, ears aloft and twitching.

She hears it, too, and her skin crawls...paws pound the earthen floor...a low growl...

Suddenly a horrific noise splits the night...a savage snarl...a human cry for help cut short...

Eyes wide, mouth set in an O of disbelief, Fisk Oeland falls backward, the beast riding him, snout to throat as the handyman gasps and weakly struggles.

"No!"

Tangled in the blanket and quilt by a nightmare not of her making, Aileen tossed and turned and fought uselessly to free herself...

She tugs at the black fur as if that could stop the destruction. A red haze glazes her view and the metallic stench of blood nearly chokes her. At last she tears the predator from its prey and throws it in the creek where she holds it until it stops struggling. The moment she lets go, it scrambles to its feet and runs off, tail between its legs.

Half his face missing, Fisk stares at her accusingly, as if somehow this is her fault.

Shaking her head in denial, she screams and the next thing she knows, Rhys is in her face, his mouth sucking the sound from hers...

Somehow Aileen tore herself from the covers and the images and out of kilter emotions that had taken over her dream space. Gasping for air and shaking despite being too warm, she tried to sort out reality from fantasy but she was simply too disturbed by all that she'd experienced.

Had this been a simple nightmare?

Or was her grandmother's legacy at work?

Act selflessly in another's behalf, and my legacy will be yours...

What had her grandmother meant by that? Act selflessly in another's behalf. It had been different for each sibling and cousin, but all had involved a life or death situation for the person they fell in love with.

Surely not. It was too late for the love part for her, she thought, even as she remembered her reaction to Rhys's kiss. A kiss that had haunted her dream.

She was so confused. How could she figure things out, stop the waking nightmare from continuing? She'd known all along that by returning to Wolf Creek she would face her own demons. But someone else's?

Act selflessly in another's behalf...

The McKenna Legacy. Her heritage. Perhaps not too late.

Another's behalf...

Rhys. Had to be. She'd thought it was the wolves, but they'd merely led her to him. What was her connection to him, the one she'd felt from the first? Did he somehow fit into her past? Had she actually met the black wolf in her dream and if so, was it one of *his?*

Her real past and present were all mixed up just as they had been in the dream turned nightmare, and Aileen knew it was up to her to unravel the thread that held the two together.

If she failed...based on the experiences of the other McKennas, Aileen feared Rhys would be doomed.

Chapter Eight

Sleep remained elusive, coming in fits and starts, Aileen fearing to let go, not knowing what she would experience if she did. By sunrise, she was wide awake.

A shower did wonders for her, as did the mug of coffee she fetched from the lobby area. Breakfast wouldn't be served for another hour, so she went back upstairs and pulled out her laptop and lost herself organizing data and searching the Internet for narratives of wolf encounters. More specifically for news of a new wolf attack.

Nothing on the wire about Fisk Oeland. Not yet. But, of course, it was only a matter of time.

Hours.

Minutes, even.

Shoulders tight, head a little achy, Aileen worked on her thesis until noon, not even realizing she'd skipped breakfast until her stomach protested. Reluctantly she got ready to go into town for lunch. Even though she hadn't found the story on the Internet yet, that didn't mean the citizens of Wolf Creek were clueless. Not only would they know about the death, they would know she had been the one to find Fisk's body.

And she needed to know what they thought about the latest incident. For her thesis. And for Rhys.

Every moment she wasn't concentrating on her work, she was thinking of the man. Of the possibilities between them. Him as her grandmother's real legacy to her. Love and danger. The dreams... the past...the sense of somehow knowing him. How would she ever connect the past to the present? What would make her remember?

When she finally went downstairs, Valerie was standing behind the front counter talking to Sheriff Caine. The owner seemed to be holding herself together. The only clue that signaled something was wrong was the tightness around the owner's mouth.

"So you have no idea what Fisk was doing out in the woods last night?"

"Why would I? I don't keep track of my employees when they leave here."

Valerie's voice was tight, as well, as if from some unnamed emotion. No doubt she'd been fond of her handyman. Aileen slowed her steps, hoping to hear more.

"I'm not trying to hassle you, Val. You know

I've always had a soft spot for you ever since that night in the fishing camp in Canada when Magnus got drunk and we got to know each other better." His voice changed as if he thought he could seduce her. "Just odd that when Fisk left here, he would head deep into the woods, which is in the opposite direction of home. You know I gotta investigate so it's clear as to who's guilty and we can take action."

So they could go after the wolves?

Not that he said it.

As if the sheriff knew Aileen was practically behind him on her way out, he turned and pinned her with his gaze. He reminded her of Rhys when he did that. She felt it physically, as if he were holding her where she stood.

"Nothing new on Fisk's death, then?" she asked.

"Not unless you're willing to talk, missy."

"I told you I didn't know anything. I just found his body."

Another moment of discomfort and he turned back to Valerie. Aileen felt as if she'd just been released from bondage. Not wanting to give the sheriff another opportunity to have at her, she rushed for the door.

"So, Val, when you gonna let me show you what it's like to be with a real man?" he asked softly.

Aileen didn't wait to hear Valerie's response.

Feeling a little nauseous, she tore outside.

In one breath the man hounded Valerie for information about her employee's death, in the next he was trying to get in her pants. She shuddered and headed for town on foot. She could use some stress-reducing exercise. And time to think.

Yesterday, Rhys had gone off to see to the wolf pack. To what end? To count noses? It had been too soon for repercussions. What had he thought to accomplish? The man's relationship with the wild pack was fascinating. And seductive. It made her want to be with him, to experience what he did with the pack.

Who was she kidding? She wanted to be with Rhys, period.

Her grandmother's legacy at work.

Unable to deny her attraction to the recluse—how could she not have soft feelings for a man determined to protect creatures that couldn't outrun human anger and fear?—Aileen snapped herself out of the reverie and took stock of her surroundings. Halfway to town, taking the shortcut Valerie had told her about when she'd arrived, she realized the forested area grew more dense, mostly with conifers. The trail got icy, too. Taking a snowmobile probably would have been a good idea, but there was no helping it now.

The pathway narrowed, the trees thickened, the light waned. A rotting log halfway across the path reminded her of finding Fisk. The short hairs at the back of her neck raised, and suddenly feeling as if eyes were watching her, she glanced back, but no one was behind her.

Nothing.

Her imagination.

Even so, she walked faster and was relieved when she hit the edge of town and the Cozy Café came into view. The feeling that someone was watching her wouldn't go away. All her senses—physical and mental—were on alert. A second sweep of the area behind her was as useless as the first.

She rushed for the café, her stomach gurgling and her pulse rushing as she opened the door and stepped inside. A dozen sets of eyes turned to her and a hush came over the diners.

They knew all right. She could tell from their grim expressions.

Balancing three plates on one arm, Liz stopped in her tracks and blinked blue-lidded eyes at her a moment before saying, "Sit anywhere you like, hon." Her voice had lost its usual cheer. "Be there to take your order in a minute."

Aileen nodded and sat at a table at the edge of the other diners. Though she picked up a menu and pretended to study it, she couldn't focus on the offerings. She could feel the stares. Curiosity or animosity? Gradually, the others went back to their meals and a toned-down conversation.

Still the words in front of her blurred, so when Liz came to take her order, Aileen assumed they served burgers and fries and asked for that.

Only after she ordered did she realize Madam Sofia was standing on the other side of the table. Wearing a flowing mahogany-red cape today, the woman looked every bit the carnival seer.

"I heard," Sofia said in a low voice. "The moon is almost full. Are you ready now?"

"For what?"

"Protection."

From werewolves?

Aileen didn't dare say it aloud, merely shook her head.

"For information, then." The strange woman leaned forward and whispered, "Wolves aren't responsible for what's happening in this area. If you're ready for the truth, come see me when you leave here."

With that, Madam Sofia made a grand exit. Not that anyone else seemed to notice. The citizens of Wolf Creek were probably all used to her eccentric ways.

Aileen found that her pulse was racing and fear

tried to take hold of her. As she thought about creeping back to her room at the lodge, she called herself every kind of coward and decided she wasn't going to hide. If she was going to ever deal with her past, she had to figure out the truth of the present, and she could start doing that by interviewing anyone who would talk to her. Needing honest opinions on the wolf-man controversy, she was certain to get them today.

Waiting until after she swallowed the last of her lunch and paid for it, Aileen stood and faced the room.

"Excuse me, but as some of you may know, I'm Aileen McKenna, a graduate student in wildlife ecology. I'm here to work on my thesis and I need your opinions about the wolf recovery program. I was hoping some of you here might be willing to talk to me, answer a few questions."

"I'm willing to tell you what I think," said a middle-aged woman from the middle of the room.

"Me, too," the man with her, probably her husband, added. "But don't be looking for no applauds for them critters, not after what happened to Fisk Oeland last night."

A murmur of agreement spread like an angry wave through the room.

"Fisk's death is under investigation," Aileen said. "But I am interested in what you have to say."

Aileen started with the couple—Abe and Sara Hanson. Turning on her recorder, she set it in the middle of the table and started asking them questions.

"How did you originally feel about wolf recovery?"

"It seemed reasonable ten, fifteen years ago," Sara said. "There weren't so many then."

"Baloney," Abe countered. "Wolves were already a problem bringing down calves and dogs as long as I can remember since I was a little kid."

Considering his age, Aileen doubted it.

Wolves had been extirpated in Wisconsin by 1960 and it wasn't until federal protection was in place that they began dispersing from Minnesota back into the state. There might be over four hundred wolves in Wisconsin now, but twenty-some years ago, when the DNR began monitoring packs through radio collars, winter tracking and summer howling surveys, there had been a mere twenty-five animals just starting to work their way down from the northern part of the state. It wasn't until the mideighties that there had been a real wolf presence.

Not that she was going to argue with the man.

"You've been compensated by the state for your losses all along though, right?"

"How do you compensate a man for not feeling safe?"

"Wolves were bothering people?"

Like they bothered her in the dream? If only she could remember it all.

"No, not people," Sara said. "I never even heard of anyone sighting a wolf this far south back then."

Except for her, Aileen thought. If she could trust the dream. But back when it had happened, she'd lost her memory and hadn't been able to tell anyone anything, certainly nothing about seeing a wolf.

"So you did lose livestock?" she asked.

"No, not me," Abe admitted, "but it could've happened to us any time."

This was the kind of unreasonable attitude that Aileen couldn't understand. But she was going to try. She kept asking questions. How had their opinions altered over the years? Had they made any changes to protect their livestock and had those changes worked? How had they modified their opinions yet again with recent deaths, which some claimed were attributable to a rogue wolf?

That last question nearly stuck in her throat. Her own thoughts had changed since she'd found Fisk. A tiny seed of doubt about all wolves being benign had crept in. She couldn't help it. She loved them, wanted to protect them. But most of all, she was afraid of them, more so now after finding Fisk's mutilated body.

There, she'd admitted it. Previously she'd tried skirting the fear issue because it had been irrational. She'd had no reason. Now it seemed—to her horror—that she had to face it head on.

"We can't turn a blind eye to what's been going on," the woman said. "Not when people are dying."

"Knute was right about hunting them critters down before we lost another good man."

"What if it was something else, though?" she asked, wondering if the word *werewolf* would be spoken.

"Like what?"

"Like they were killed, but not by a wolf."

"You mean murder?"

"Sure," she said, going along with the woman's suggestion, wondering where this would lead. "Did Fisk Oeland or Tom Patterson or the others before them have any enemies?"

The café went silent like it had when she'd walked in the door. Aileen felt herself start to sweat. She hadn't been thinking of murder, but what if…

"If you want to be taken seriously," Abe said, "don't try to excuse them wolves. We all know how dangerous they are. C'mon, Sara, let's stop wasting our time."

The Hansons left and no one else would talk to her except for an elderly lady who'd come in a few minutes before and had only a cup of tea on the table. The woman had been born in Wolf Creek and had never lived anywhere else.

"The wolves keep me company now that my husband is gone," she said, a wistful note in her voice.

Suddenly, Aileen became aware of someone staring at her back. A wolf hater, no doubt. She tried to shake away the uncomfortable feeling.

"You see the wolves?" she asked.

"Hear them. I live right outside of town and on a clear night I pretend they're singing to me."

"You're not afraid of them, then?"

The woman smiled sadly and shook her head. "All that talk of wolf kills is nonsense."

"So you don't believe Tom Patterson and Fisk Oeland were victims of a wolf."

"Fisk?" the woman repeated, her gaze shifting to a spot over Aileen's shoulder. "Something happened to Fisk now?"

So the whole town *didn't* know. Somehow the woman had remained oblivious to the town's newest tragedy.

The back of her neck grew hot and Aileen

turned to find Rhys standing there, staring at her. Her stomach did a little flip and the breath squeezed out of her chest. Unable to focus, she quickly wrapped up the interview with the elderly woman who was still mumbling about poor Fisk. Not knowing what else to do, Aileen patted her hand, told her how sorry she was and thanked her for her time.

Rhys tilted his head, indicated she should step outside with him. Thinking he knew more about Fisk's death, she went willingly, slipping into her jacket as she moved. When she brushed by him, she felt his energy surround her as if it were a tangible thing. Her pulse sped up and her breath felt labored once more.

Outside the diner, however, Aileen was brought up short by Rhys's disapproving expression. Two men moved along the sidewalk toward them. Sheriff Caine and Knute Oeland. They seemed to be arguing. The only word she caught was Knute's nastily spat *wolves*. The sheriff patted the man on the shoulder. With his brother dead, no doubt Knute was demanding action before the coroner even finished his report.

Rhys pulled her between buildings, out of their way. But the two men didn't come past them—they entered the diner. Aileen realized the sheriff had spotted them and was surprised he hadn't stopped to hassle her again. Maybe because she was with Rhys.

"Great timing." Rhys's tone was low but gruff as he asked, "Are you out of your mind? What are you thinking, stirring up the debate over the wolves right now? What if I hadn't pulled you out of there before Knute walked in?"

"I'm doing what I came here to do. I still have a thesis to write." She wasn't about to tell him that she was looking for answers about the past as well as the present. That she was trying to remember, trying to make connections. That she was equally worried about him.

"Circumstances have changed."

"And I'm gathering fresh reactions to the circumstances," she said. "Whatever my opinion, I would be remiss if I let it go."

That was true. To write her thesis, she needed to be a sieve and let information flow through her before drawing conclusions. Shaping the document in the direction she chose was tempting, but not particularly scholarly. Besides, she was looking for some real truths, not just answers to back up her own opinions, which had grown a bit shaky in the last twenty-four hours.

"You're going to get yourself killed."

The way Rhys was looking at her, all concerned and protective, made Aileen soften toward him. He had her best interests at heart, after all. Apparently she meant something to him, as well.

"What?" she asked. "You think a wolf is going to follow me home and kill me?"

"That's not funny."

"It's not meant to be."

"You're serious?" Rhys's frown deepened. "You think—"

"After yesterday, I don't know what to think. I'm looking for explanations."

"Well you're not going to find them here."

"Did *you* find them?" she asked. "When you left me, you went back to protect the pack. But did you get any answers?"

"Not yet."

"Nothing about the autopsy?"

She figured he probably had connections, either with the DNR representative he'd been chatting up or with Sheriff Caine, that if anyone could find out what had happened to Fisk in less than twenty-four hours, it would be Rhys.

He said, "Nothing conclusive."

"What does that mean?"

Rhys scowled. "The coroner is leaning toward a wolf having killed Oeland."

"Not that I want it to be true," Aileen said. "Exactly the opposite. But what if he's right?"

"He isn't."

"Then can you explain what you think happened?" she asked. "Surely you must have a theory."

Aileen swore Rhys blanched. A moment passed. And then another. There was something he wasn't telling her. She was certain of it.

Finally, he said, "Look, something I can't explain is going on here. Be careful of what you say to Sheriff Caine especially. I heard him tell the coroner to find another explanation for Oeland's death."

"Maybe because he doesn't believe it was a wolf kill."

"Because he doesn't want the feds interfering. And maybe something else…"

"Like what?"

Rhys stared at her and for a moment Aileen thought he was about to illuminate her. In the end, he shook his head as though he'd changed his mind.

"Like murder?" she asked.

"You didn't suggest that in there?" he asked, indicating the café.

"As a matter of fact, I did. What if it's true, Rhys? What if someone had reason to kill these men and then let some animal loose on them to cover his tracks?"

A more rational idea than Sofia Zak's werewolf theory.

Rhys swore softly, then said, "Why don't you just let me get you out of here." He took her by the arm but she resisted. "I'm thinking about your safety. It's not the wolves that worry me, it's the people in this town. You don't know who heard you in there, or how many people will carry the tale to others."

"So you think it might be true?" she asked. "You think it'll get back to the killer and then he'll be after me?"

"What's happening here isn't natural, Aileen."

"Not usual, you mean."

"Not *natural* as the citizens of this town would define such," he said with emphasis. "There are other forces in this world…"

He shook his head, but he didn't go on.

Nevertheless, Aileen's breath caught in her throat. What was he trying to tell her? Madam Sofia's warning came back to her. Surely not.

"Don't tell me you believe in werewolves?" she joked. But what if that *was* what he meant?

Rhys didn't answer her, merely stepped closer, seared the side of her face with his fingertips and leaned in so that his lips nearly brushed her cheek when he said, "I don't want anything to happen to you."

Fire trailed down her neck, and she nearly melted into him. Her lips burned and her breasts swelled, both wanting his touch. How could she resist a man who wanted to protect her from harm? But what if it was she who had to protect him?

Act selflessly in another's behalf…

Aileen pressed her hand against his chest in an attempt to give herself breathing room, but a strong arm around her back and a steady gaze held her fast. His quickened heartbeat made her move her hand into something solid. A quick glance down showed it to be a stuffed leather pouch hanging from a leather thong, one she'd never seen him wear before. The beading made her wonder if it was some Native American charm. Staring into Rhys's eyes, she felt her senses sharpen her awareness of him as a man. His scent…his heat…his power. All alpha.

She wanted to get even closer, to feel him twined around and through her…the two of them as one…never to be separated.

For a moment he made her forget fear…forget danger…forget death.

Hunger that had nothing to do with food dominated her, made her feel an electric connection along every nerve and Aileen thought if Rhys wanted to take her right there, on the street, she would let him.

As if he could read her thoughts, Rhys went wide-eyed. And stepped back.

It took everything Aileen had to keep steady and not let her knees give way.

"I'll see you back to the lodge," he offered. Quietly this time. Still with the same power.

Her pulse continuing to thrum in the same strange rhythm, she said, "I'm not ready to go back."

"Then I'll wait."

"No. There's something I have to do. Alone."

"I don't like it."

This time Aileen chose silence, and while Rhys tried to stare her down, she was determined to do what she must…which meant she couldn't let him dominate her. Finally, he nodded and backed away.

"I'll call you later, let you know I'm all right." Her concession didn't take the wrinkle from Rhys's brow, so Aileen tried to soften him. "If you want, you can meet me at the lodge later."

"Not tonight," he said immediately. His tone almost harsh, he clarified, "Not a good idea."

If he hadn't added the last comment, she would simply have thought he had plans. But obviously it was something else. Certain she would get no explanation, she didn't pursue it. Instead she moved off, leaving him standing there looking after her as she headed toward Pine Street.

"Look to your own back, wolf man," she murmured.

If he wouldn't give her any reasonable answers, perhaps Madam Sofia would.

Chapter Nine

"So you are finally coming to terms with reality." Madam Sofia's lips turned up in a rueful smile, showing the gap in her front teeth.

"Reality?" Aileen echoed. "I don't have a clue what that might be."

"If that were true, you wouldn't be here."

Madam Sofia came out from behind the counter and indicated Aileen should follow. Her velvet dress glowed red-black against the deepening gloom of the shop. The eccentric woman certainly liked her drama.

They passed through a curtain of glass beads into a back room, which was set up like a parlor. A round lace-covered table was set with two cups and saucers and spoons. A woodburning stove kept the chill from the air and heated a kettle that whistled softly.

"I thought you might like some tea." Madam Sofia placed a previously prepared teapot on the table and filled it with hot water. "Make yourself comfortable. Sit."

Appreciating the aroma that immediately filled the air, Aileen hung her jacket on the back of the chair and did as the woman suggested.

"Apparently you were that certain I would come."

"You have so many questions."

"And you have the answers?"

"Many of them. Not all."

Did she really know the truth about the deaths? Aileen wondered, though she asked, "Have you shared your information with the authorities?"

The woman laughed. "They wouldn't appreciate the truth. Or believe it."

"Then why do you think I will?"

"Because you already know."

Aileen snorted. "You think I believe in werewolves?" That had to be the woman's point.

Pouring steaming liquid into the two cups the color of amber, like Rhys's eyes, Madam Sofia asked, "Isn't that why you had to come back, because of what happened to you here when you were a girl?"

Aileen's pulse kick-started. "You didn't live here back then. What do you know about that?"

"What do you remember?"

Realizing she was going to have to give something to get something in return, Aileen said, "Not much. Bits and pieces have started coming back since I returned here, but I don't know what is real and what isn't."

"Trust your dreams."

How did the other woman know about them? Aileen wondered. She would put it to the self-proclaimed seer's being a good guesser—to her being able to read body language and expressions—but Madam Sofia had been the one to bring Aileen's past up out of nowhere.

"I can't trust my dreams. They're all mixed up. They don't make sense."

"Yet they hold the truth. You merely have to look deeper, get past the barriers that you yourself put up."

Easier said than done, as far as Aileen was concerned.

"Drink your tea before it gets cold."

Madam Sofia picked up her cup and sipped, so Aileen did the same. The brew smelled fragrant, but the hot liquid left a faint bitter aftertaste.

"What did you put in here?" she immediately asked. Surely nothing terrible since Madam Sofia was drinking it also.

"Nothing to hurt you. Only some herbs."

Eyeing the cup suspiciously, Aileen put it down. "One of your potions?"

"You could call it that."

"To what end?"

"It will offer you some measure of protection." Madam Sofia raised her cup and took another sip.

"Back to the werewolves?"

"Werewolves…lycanthropes…shape-shifters… they've always existed. Stories of human-animal transformations are worldwide…timeless."

"Stories, right."

"You scoff at what you do not understand."

"Then enlighten me."

"The killings started more than twenty years ago, even before the wolves migrated this far south," Sofia said. "The victims came from a wider network, but the pattern followed the wolf migration."

Aileen realized Madam Sofia was intimating that generations had somehow been involved, since the average life span of a gray wolf in the wild was six to eight years.

"I thought you were working in some carnival until recent years."

"That I was, but we went everywhere in several states, including to northern Wisconsin. But Wolf Creek has always been my home, and I was drawn back here from time to time."

"Still, there were no reports of deaths potentially attributed to wolves until recently," Aileen reminded her.

"The victims were simply better hidden. Or perhaps the evidence was eaten...bones and all."

Aileen's initial response to the last remark was a shudder that ran up her spine.

"Or perhaps there were no victims," Aileen suggested, "and you're simply trying to scare me so I'll buy one of your potions."

"I don't want your money. Part of you believes, or you would be gone. Every time I returned to this area over the years, I smelled evil on the wind, and my visions showed me the truth."

Where was the woman going with this? Aileen wondered. Madam Sofia had her visions...and McKennas had their gifts, she in the form of dreams. Something *had* happened to her. Something she was starting to remember.

"The truth," Aileen echoed softly. "Like what happened to me when I was a girl?"

But Madam Sofia was one step removed from the room. Her eyes had gone unfocused and her voice sounded strange as she said, "I saw the transformations...the kills...the burials..." as if she were seeing them right this minute.

Then the old woman shook her head and gave a drawn-out sigh that sent another chill through Aileen. She suddenly had the cup in hand and had to decide whether or not to drink. Whether or not to believe.

She took a sip, and, her pulse humming, asked, "Are you saying that something like that happened to me? Something my mind tucked away for all these years?"

Sofia's gaze focused on Aileen. "Haven't you wondered why you are so drawn to Rhys Lindgren? Other than the obvious." Her eyes sparkled and a smile crossed her lips. "I might be old, but I still have an eye for the beautiful man. What the two of you experience together goes beyond that. Beyond normal. You must feel it."

Not liking the sense that the woman was in her skin—more than that, not liking the intimation about Rhys—Aileen asked, "What aren't you telling me?"

"What you need to remember on your own."

Frustration made Aileen want to shout. If Madam Sofia knew what had happened to her all those years ago, why didn't she just come out with it? Convinced confrontation wouldn't get her the answers she needed, she took a deep breath and concentrated on relaxing.

"And you never shared any of this werewolf information with anyone before?" Aileen asked. "Why me?"

"Because I couldn't convince nonbelievers.

Why you? Because you know…because you can stop it."

Aileen's breath caught in her throat. Sofia was serious. The old woman really believed in were-wolves and expected Aileen to do so, as well. Not only that, she apparently expected Aileen to do something about stopping the deaths.

"Free yourself from what you think you know, Aileen McKenna. Not all in this world is ruled by science. There are many things we can't explain." Madam Sofia reached out and touched Aileen's hand. "But you would know that because you are a sensitive. You have the gift, even if you haven't explored it fully. If you're different, why not others? Who is to say the extent of the world's mysteries?"

Feeling herself slipping, Aileen tried to hold tight onto what she thought of as reality, but she simply couldn't. Madam Sofia was correct. All her life, she'd been apathetic about the gift she'd inherited from her grandmother. She accepted the dreams as her heritage and yet never had explored them to find out where she could take them. And in the last several years, Donovan and their McKenna cousins had accepted their destinies. They'd lived through experiences that had chilled her, that had made her want to forget about anything supernatural.

Supernatural…not natural…

That's what Rhys had claimed that very afternoon. He hadn't explained. Because he feared she would think he was crazy? If she had pressed him, would he have brought up the possibility of a werewolf being responsible for the deaths? Were he and Madam Sofia on the same page?

"Let yourself believe, Aileen. If you do, you can save the creatures…and the people…you love."

Act selflessly in another's behalf…

Is this what she needed to do to save Rhys? Aileen wondered, needed to accept what she'd believed was myth?

"Where do these supernatural creatures come from?" Aileen asked. "Where do they hide?"

"Werewolves can be made either by magic or by bite, but only during a full moon. And the person may die before turning if there's too great a blood loss. The threat in this area came from the far north, migrating from Canada like the wolves. Perhaps alongside them. They don't need to hide from us. On the move, they look to be wolves, although perhaps bigger. Most of the time, though, they can simply blend in with us."

"You mean live among us?"

"Side by side. And unless you caught one when the full moon rose, you might never know."

"I don't understand."

"A powerful lycanthrope can turn at any time he or she chooses. The closer to the full moon, the harder it is to resist the pull. Can't you feel it?" Sofia looked around as if she could see the charge in the very air. "The full moon is the only time the creature can't resist the change. Unless it's protected, of course."

"Protected. As by a potion?"

"A potion…herbs…a spell…Wolfsbane or aconite, a kind of buttercup, is particularly effective. It can be poisonous if ingested. It can repel a werewolf if a human is wearing it…or if worn on a werewolf in human form, it can keep it from turning."

"And you can provide wolfsbane?"

"If a werewolf came to me and asked for help, yes."

"Why would one do so?" Aileen asked, as if she did believe.

"Being a lycanthrope in itself doesn't make the creature evil, but it does need to feed. If it remembers what it did when in animal form—though that doesn't always happen—it may be horrified by its own actions if the kill was human. It may want to prevent the change."

"How do you know all this? Has a werewolf come to you for help?"

Madam Sofia hesitated for a moment, then said. "No werewolf…not here…not exactly."

Wondering exactly what she did mean with the roundabout answer, Aileen mused, "Not a werewolf. A real wolf?"

Madam Sofia sighed. "As I said, there are more permutations to the life in this universe than you understand now. But unless you leave Wolf Creek…unless you leave your responsibility… you will come to know it all."

Could Madam Sofia be any more vague?

Aileen decided now was the time to be direct herself. "If there are lycanthropes among us, would you mind pointing out who they might be?"

"You don't need me to do so. Look beyond the external form, Aileen McKenna, and you will recognize the true nature of the beast."

Enough was enough. A frustrated Aileen got to her feet and prepared to leave. "Thank you for the lesson in mysticism," she said politely.

"I know you don't mean that now, but soon, you will." Rising, Madam Sofia took something from her pocket and pressed it into Aileen's hand. "Whether or not you believe, please keep this on you at all times. No charge. The moon will soon again be full."

Aileen opened her palm. Nestled there was a

small beaded leather pouch surrounding a capped glass vial. "What is it?"

"A tincture containing wolfsbane. Keep it on your person and it will protect you. Ingested, the contents will keep a werewolf from turning."

"I thought you said wolfsbane was poison."

"The tincture is diluted wolfsbane. I would never dispense anything strong enough to kill. That would be against my coven's canons."

Coven…so she considered herself a witch. Aileen's head ached. She wasn't about to get into another level of the supernatural.

"If this isn't poison, then how am I supposed to stop the werewolf?"

"You'll find a way."

Great. She'd come to Madam Sofia for answers and she was leaving the old woman's shop with more questions.

THOUGH IT WAS NOT EVEN five o'clock, the sun had set. Aileen realized they were nearing the winter solstice with the longest night of the year. A pagan holiday. Would Madam Sofia and her coven celebrate then? Would they have reason to?

As she walked back to Main Street, the moon was already rising in the night sky and casting a blue glow over the snow-covered earth. Some of the shops and businesses had already closed, and others would soon do the same. She hadn't meant to stay away from the lodge so late.

Hurrying along, she thought about Rhys, about the attraction Sofia had said was beyond normal. The old woman had been right about that. Maybe she was right about a lot of things.

Stopping at the edge of town, Aileen pulled the leather pouch from her pocket and took a better look. The beading seemed familiar…similar to the beading on the leather pouch Rhys had been wearing earlier. Undoubtedly, he'd gone to see Madam Sofia himself. A thought that made her spine prickle.

Starting off on the shortcut from town to the lodge, Aileen couldn't help being preoccupied, going over the old woman's claims. And since Rhys wore the protection Madam Sofia had given him, he must believe in the supernatural. No wonder he'd been reading the book about were-wolves.

Aileen looked up through the thicket of trees to the night sky. Indeed, the moon was almost full. A shiver coursed through her and she glanced back at the fading light from town, which suddenly seemed so far away.

Why hadn't she taken the damn snowmobile?

Hurrying on, she thought again of Rhys and wondered if he wore the leather pouch because he knew something she didn't, a possibility she'd considered several times.

Rhys hung around the pack. What if a werewolf did also, as Madam Sofia had suggested? Had Rhys seen it? Did he recognize it for what it was? Did he know the identity of the man who changed into a wolf?

The identity of the murderer?

Her pulse picked up a beat at the thought, though knowing and proving were two different things.

A shush of snow from somewhere nearby made Aileen suspect someone else was using the shortcut. Another glance back assured her that no one was behind her, and yet, she couldn't relax. The oddest feeling—like a hostile gaze tracking her—made her move faster. And then she heard another noise—a low rumble that raised the hair at the back of her neck. Someone was there, just out of sight.

Someone or *something?*

Damn Madam Sofia for scaring her!

Her mouth went dry and her throat tightened as she hurried on, now tuned into the night.

Were those footsteps she heard? Or her imagination? No, they were real.

Her stomach clenched and Aileen fumbled in her pocket and wrapped shaky fingers around the pouch that was supposed to protect her. She pulled it out and pressed her hand to her chest. Moving so fast that she was almost skating on the slippery path, she could hardly breathe as the sounds inched closer.

Footsteps…no!…paws hitting the earth…

Was that a low growl?

The blood rushing through her head muffled the sounds as something flew through the brush toward her, banged the back of her shoulder and knocked her to her knees. As she tried to catch herself, the pouch flew from her fingers. With a shriek, Aileen got to her feet and scrabbled forward. She grabbed for the pouch, but her fingers nicked the edge and it skidded out of reach.

Once.

Twice!

Finally she got her fingers around the leather and made a fist. As she turned to face her attacker, she held it out in front of her.

No one was there.

Starting to ease backward down the trail, Aileen jerked her gaze from one side to the other—the hand holding the charm following. At any second, she expected something would jump out at her from the bushes again.

Someone or something had been there, had knocked her to her knees.

She hadn't imagined it. Had she?

Could she have been so frightened by her conversation with Madam Sofia that she had created the danger in her own mind?

A nearby howl set her short hairs to attention, and the thud of something hitting the wet earth drove her around into a full-out run for her life. She could see the lodge's lights through the trees, just ahead.

Just a little farther. She could make it.

Her heart felt as if it were about to burst from her chest when she caught movement from the corner of her left eye and a dark shape darted at her.

Flipping around, she tried to veer off too late.

Struck hard, she kept to her feet, clung to the pouch and prayed.

Chapter Ten

"Aah!"

Valerie Gleiter jumped back, looking as terrified and off balance as Aileen felt. Her heart in
her throat, Aileen gasped and steadied herself as
relief washed through her.

"Sorry, sorry," Aileen choked out.

"Me, too. My word, you scared me!" Valerie
said, wrapping her arms around her middle.
"Why in the world were you running like that?"

"I thought someone was following me."

Taking a good look behind Aileen, Valerie
grabbed her by the arm as if she was going to
pull her toward the lodge, but just as suddenly
let go and backed off. "I don't see anything, but
let's get inside."

Though she threw a nervous look over her
shoulder, Aileen followed the other woman.
"Whatever it was…or whoever…it's gone."

"Finding Fisk must have been traumatic." The

normally distant lodge owner sounded on edge. "I'm sure your nerves are shaky. The imagination is a powerful thing."

Aileen didn't believe she'd imagined her pursuer. In the morning, she intended to go back to that shortcut and look for tracks—human or otherwise—because she had to know what had been after her.

Not that she was in any mood to argue.

Once they were both inside, Valerie locked the door and stood at the windows staring out. She seemed nearly as nervous as Aileen was feeling. And who could blame her considering the circumstance?

Still, Aileen not only sensed Valerie's strength, but she could also see it when the other woman straightened and turned her back to the windows.

"You look like you could use a drink," Valerie said, stripping off her gloves, then her jacket. "I know I could. Why don't you wait for me over there by the fire. I'll get us some brandy from my office. We can sit and talk until you feel better."

"Sure." Undoubtedly Valerie needed the company, as well. "Thanks."

Realizing she was still gripping the leather pouch, Aileen relaxed and put it back in her pocket.

Was it possible the wolfsbane had saved her, had kept a werewolf from attacking her?

Was it possible she was a little crazy tonight?

The moment she took off her coat, Aileen remembered her promise to call Rhys. She found her cell, but the call went to voice mail.

"Hey, Rhys. I'm back at the lodge, so you can stop worrying." Now *she* could worry. Why hadn't he answered his phone when she'd told him she would call? "Call me when you get in, would you? Something followed me home tonight and I'm not sure it was human."

Shivering, she moved in close to the fire and absorbed its warmth until Valerie came out from her office carrying two brandy snifters.

"Here you go." Valerie handed her one.

"Thanks. A double?"

"I figured we could use it." Valerie clanked her glass to Aileen's. "To better—and safer—times."

"Cheers."

Aileen took a small sip. She rarely drank hard liquor, so after the brandy burned its way down her throat, she contented herself with swirling the amber liquid and staring down into the bowl of her glass.

"You seem to be deep in thought."

"I have a lot to think about." Aileen met Valerie's gaze and took another sip before setting down the snifter. "I interviewed some of the people in town for my thesis. And I went to Caravan Herbs and Potions."

"Ah, Madam Sofia. Did the witch scare you, too?"

The old woman had scared Valerie? Surprising. "Sort of. She doesn't think wolves are responsible for the recent deaths. She blames a werewolf."

"Really?"

Aileen hiccuped a nervous laugh. "I'm too naive and she can be very convincing. I half believe her."

Valerie's response was to slug down some of the brandy. Okay, so did she know something she wasn't saying? Aileen wondered.

"You don't believe her, do you, Valerie? I mean it's just myth, right? She probably gets her ideas from all those books and movies that have been out recently."

"I only wish we were dealing with myth." Valerie's gaze was steady when she met Aileen's, almost as if she were testing her. "But too many things that can't be explained have been happening. It makes everyone wonder."

Great. She'd brought up the subject because it was all too much for her to take in and she'd turned to Valerie for common sense. Instead the lodge owner seemed to agree with Madam Sofia. Aileen couldn't shake the feeling that whatever had chased her was still out there.

Waiting…

She stared through the atrium windows, but the forest beyond was dark. The moon hid behind clouds. Was there someone—something—staring at them in return?

"I don't get the feeling you were meant to live in such an isolated place," Valerie said, interrupting her morbid musings. "I can see that it has already gotten the better of you. If you wanted to check out early, I wouldn't hold you to your reservation."

"I have a commitment to stay. A new career. Just like you have this lodge."

"Right. The lodge." Valerie took another swallow of brandy, a big one. "Trust me, if I could get rid of it, I would go in a heartbeat."

"Then why don't you? This is prime property."

"Which I can't sell for years to come. When I was young and foolish, I met and fell in love with Magnus Gleiter, a well-to-do entrepreneur from northern Canada. I became who he wanted…and now I'm stuck here."

Valerie sounded lonely and scared and Aileen wondered if she was one of those women who'd gotten her identity from her husband—*she became what he wanted*—and now that he was dead she was lost. But having seen the other woman in action, it was hard to imagine her in that position.

"I'm sorry your husband is gone but—"

"Well, I'm not!" Valerie snapped, shocking Aileen. "I married him under false pretenses. I didn't really know who Magnus was when I met him, or how cruel and manipulative he could be when I married him. By the time I figured it out, it was too late."

An abused wife, Aileen realized. Who would have thought it of a woman like Valerie? Then again, some women lost their heads when it came to a man.

Aileen asked, "What about family?"

"None to speak of though I always hoped for a family of my own, of course, but I've been denied that—I've had several miscarriages." Valerie's fingers tightened on her glass. "Still, I haven't lost hope. I simply need to be with the right man to father my children."

An odd way to put it, but Aileen got her drift, couldn't help but think of Rhys. "I can't wait to have my own kids." Seeing Willow had brought on the yearning. "But the right man to father them isn't easy to find."

"Magnus sure wasn't it." Valerie's voice was bitter. "He changed my world and I was helpless to change it back. Now I have no choice, nowhere else to go. My resources are limited. Even though they found blood around my husband's campsite, they never found his body. Magnus can't be legally declared dead yet, and everything is tied up in the lodge. So unless a miracle happens, I'm stuck with this place and a life of isolation for years to come."

Remembering the sheriff coming on to Valerie, indicating they'd had some kind of tryst in Canada, Aileen said, "Sheriff Caine seems kind of sweet on you."

Valerie shuddered. "I don't think so."

"I'm sorry. I hope you can find whatever it is that you do need, then."

"Thanks. You're a good listener."

Aileen smiled. "Good thing. I'll have to do a lot of that in my work."

"And this really is where you want to work?"

"It's where my work will be. Not exactly here in Wolf Creek, perhaps, but someplace like this."

"So you'll be trapped, too."

"If I hate it, I can always go back to Chicago. I do have family and friends there. Surely you can do something to get away from here if you're so unhappy. Maybe let a manager handle the lodge?"

"Then the income wouldn't be enough to live on. Not well enough, anyway. Being broke for years until Magnus can be declared dead holds no appeal, and the only thing I know how to do is run this place."

"That's a lot. You seem like a strong woman, Valerie. I would bet you can do anything you set your mind to."

"I'll drink to that. Actually, I'll drink to all women finding their strength, whatever that might be."

Valerie emptied her brandy glass and Aileen took a last sip from hers.

And a last look out the lodge windows.

Despite the fact that the moon was almost full, there was nothing to see—the moon must be hidden under a cloud cover and fresh snow clung to the glass.

Still, as she picked up her things to go to her room, Aileen couldn't fight the feeling that the night had eyes.

FLESH CRAWLS ALONG HER SPINE. She whips around to see a snarling golden-brown wolf break from the fog-shrouded trees. She's never feared an animal before, but now her heart threatens to beat right out of her chest.

Its glowing yellow gaze pins her...

Gasping with fear, she runs.

She's hit from behind and she lands hard on hands and knees. The animal's weight presses into her back, and desperately, she tries to shake it off but can't.

Its breath is hot and wet on her neck...

Aileen opened her eyes and stared into the dark of her room and checked it out. No glowing yellow eyes gazed back at her. Sighing with relief, she let her tired lids droop closed, then moved her fingers under the pillow until they surrounded the pouch. Silly, perhaps, but she felt better knowing the talisman was there.

The past, she thought, *remember the past.*

Madam Sofia said she could do it.

She kept repeating that mantra to herself over and over until she drifted off...

Another jolt frees her of the deadly load—the black wolf to her rescue!

Crying now, she watches from the ground as the two animals tumble together in a vicious, snarling battle—bodies tangled, jaws snapping, wounds and spurting blood making them cry out in near-human shrieks. The black wolf sinks his teeth into the brown's neck. Frantic, the trapped wolf kicks and writhes itself free, skitters away back toward the stand of firs, tail between its legs.

For a moment, it hesitates and looks back defiantly before disappearing into the forest.

The black wolf stands in front of her as if on guard...and then with a pitiful whimper, slowly sinks to its haunches, and then down-down-down to the earth, collapsing on its side next to her...

This time when she awoke, Aileen felt her heart thump against her ribs as if the attack were happening now and she was in the middle.

The dream echoed in part what she'd experienced earlier—being hit from behind and then falling. Plus, it had turned into another confused dream...or had it really happened? Had one wolf attacked her and another protected her on that night whose memory she had buried for so many years?

It would explain a lot. Her love/fear of wolves, certainly. Her fear of the forest.

What it didn't explain was her willingness to indulge in fantasy.

Aileen pulled the pouch from under the pillow and studied the beading, ran her fingertip over the cap on the vial. Did the tincture of wolfsbane inside really have protective powers? If Madam Sofia hadn't given it to her, would she have made it home safely? What would have happened to her if she'd refused to take the pouch?

What would have happened all those years ago if the black wolf hadn't come to her rescue? The wolf had been wounded instead of her. Had it died?

Certain there was more to that night so long ago, Aileen settled back and breathed deeply to slow her pulse...to let herself go...to see the rest...

Deep...deep...deep in the dark forest, she looks for the black wolf, but he's nowhere to be seen. She's whole. Not bruised. Not a child.

She senses a presence. Danger. It surrounds her.

She must escape.

Feeling as if her heart were about to burst, she runs and runs, but can't outrun sounds that frighten her. Scrabbling. Growling. The rapid crunching of snow.

It's coming for her.

Catching up to her.

But when she flies around and holds out the wolfsbane to drive off the danger, Rhys is there. He looks wounded...sad as if he were disappointed in her. He pushes aside the hand holding the protection and steps into her and once more she feels his heat surround and enter her.

He nuzzles her neck...laves it with his tongue... tests the delicate flesh with his teeth...

Her knees grow weak and she drops the pouch and hangs on to him hard, ready to give over to him until he pulls back, his amber eyes glowing in the face of a black wolf.

"What the...!"

Heart pounding, Aileen sits up in bed and forces herself awake, the depth of her growing confusion evident in her dream state.

She is beastly hot…sexually aroused. Her nipples jut against the thin silky material of her nightgown. Wet warmth pools between her thighs. Rhys has the power to do that to her, even in a dream.

Even wearing the face of a wolf.

Aileen slips out of bed. Thinking to let the outside air soothe her, she opens the door to the deck. An immediate scrabbling sound raises the flesh along her spine, but before she can react, she glimpses Rhys on the deck getting to his feet. Snow falls and he wears a light cloak of white.

Opening the door, she asks, "What are you doing out there?"

"Standing guard. Making sure you're safe."

"How did you get up here?" she asks, looking at the steep drop to the ground.

"I jumped."

She tries to imagine a leap that huge. She can't. "You said you couldn't see me tonight."

"I didn't think it wise."

"Why?"

"Don't you know? I'm no good for you."

She is standing on the snow-covered deck in bare feet and a skimpy gown, but she's never felt hotter. Her breasts swell and the fluid thickens between her thighs.

"Why?" she asks, moving closer. "Why aren't

you good for me? What happened to me when I was a girl? You know, don't you?"

His features become sharp. Intense. But he shakes his head. "I know you," he says. "I recognize your scent. But I don't know why."

She feels driven to press him. She comes closer, barely leaving breathing room between them. He might as well be touching her. The experience is extraordinary. She feels him as if he were part of her. As if they were halves of a whole.

"What would it take," she says softly, bending her head so her hair falls across his cheek, "to make you remember?"

"You should go in. It's not safe out here."

"Why? What's the danger?"

"I'm the danger," he says, shooting a thrill down to her snow-covered toes.

"I know. You make me afraid...but you won't drive me off. I think..." she reaches out and touches his chest where the leather pouch dangles "...that you might be my legacy...I think...that I could love you..."

For a moment, she doesn't think he will react. Then in a head-spinning second, he scoops her up into him and kisses her like no man has ever kissed her before, as if he's claiming his right of possession. She lets him and returns his passion.

Her world shifts and she clings to him to stay

upright. Sensation courses through her, lighting every nerve in her body. He whirls her around, presses her against the railing. She spreads her thighs and nudges him. A moment later, his hand touches her there in her most secret place, his fingers sliding in and out along the liquid trail so that she sees stars inside her head.

No, no, the stars are above them. Arching her back, she can see them between snowflakes.

The night shines in a way it never has before. The glow fills her heart. Her soul. She looks deep into Rhys's eyes and sees there a like feeling for her.

Is it love?

With a trembling hand, she releases the catch on his pants and opens him to her questing fingers. Circling him, she slips her hand to his tip and then down to his groin. His groan fills her head and she can't stop from guiding him to her entrance. Wanting to be part of him, wanting them to be two halves of a whole, she fills herself with him, sliding down, taking him all in, losing herself in the immediate response of her flesh. Wrapping her legs around his hips, she leans back so that he can suckle her breasts as she urges him in deeper, in her mind's eye seeing them become one, forever inseparable…

Heart pounding, Aileen sat up in bed and forced

herself awake, through her confused dream state. She was so hot...and sexually aroused. Rhys had the power to do that to her, even in a dream.

Even wearing the face of a wolf.

Wait!

Her thoughts and actions were scarily familiar. She'd dreamed this before, dreamed of making love to Rhys. Hadn't she?

Dawn filtered into the chilly room and Aileen realized the deck door was cracked open.

Getting out of bed to shut it, she felt as if her body had recently been well-used. Her breasts were tender, as was the flesh between her thighs.

Almost as if she'd had sex while dreaming rather than dreaming about having sex...

Her pulse threaded. No, that couldn't be right, not unless she'd been sleepwalking again. That hadn't happened for years. So why did she feel this inner contentment, this romantic afterglow from what undoubtedly had been a dream? Why did she want to shout to the world that she'd experienced something that until now had been elusive and unreal to her?

Love...was she really in love? Or was that part of a dream, too?

Rather than closing and locking the deck door, she opened it wide and stepped outside to see for herself if there was evidence of a tryst.

The deck and rail were covered with fresh snow. No imprints indicating an intimate encounter. What was wrong with her? Why did she feel like she'd had the best sexual experience of her life? Why was she in a state of euphoria? Why couldn't she get Rhys out of mind?

Suddenly chilled to the bone, she shivered and backed into the room. But not before she saw evidence that someone—something—had been on the deck not so long ago. They were almost buried by the newly falling snow, but the outlines were still there.

Footprints…not human…animal…

Prints she would swear had been left by a wolf.

Chapter Eleven

Wondering where the boy had been half the night, Jens watched Rhys suck up his breakfast like it had been aeons since he'd eaten. Or like he didn't know when or where he was going to get his next meal. He hadn't seen him like this since he'd first brought him home.

"Your appetite's picked up."

"I'm feeling better." Rhys took a swallow of coffee, then, fork poised over his food, said, "I'm going over to Gray Wolf Lodge to ask Valerie Gleiter for work. Now that Fisk Oeland is dead, she needs a new man around the place to help her out, especially with the holidays."

That announcement was enough to make Jens lose his appetite.

"I don't like it," he muttered, throwing his fork down on his plate.

Rhys shoveled in bacon and a hunk of scrambled egg. "It's only temporary."

"It's because of the McKenna woman, isn't it?" Jens had known she was trouble from the first. He'd tried to warn Rhys, but the boy hadn't listened.

"Partly," Rhys agreed, for a moment looking like a besotted fool. "But we are isolated, and if I'm ever going to figure out what's going on…Aileen suggested it might be murder, someone covering his tracks by making it look like a wolf kill. She may be right, but I can't do anything sitting here. I need a way to get information."

Jens had kept the boy isolated for a reason, and Rhys had never before defied him. Men had died, but Rhys hadn't put himself in jeopardy to sort it out until the McKenna woman had gotten herself in the mix.

"You think you'll get information out of Valerie Gleiter?" he asked.

"Her or others."

"Be careful, son. What if she wants you to move in?"

Rhys fingered the leather pouch dangling from his neck. "You were right about my going to Madam Sofia. No more uncontrollable urges. I can keep things in check. And I remember everything that happened last night."

"That was only one night. It's going to get worse when the moon is full. I know you wouldn't do anything terrible no matter what, but you could still get into trouble if you're out wandering around at night."

"I'll be all right. If I need to, I'll come back here."

Assuming he would be able to do so. Jens wasn't so sure. Something could go wrong.

He adjusted his thick glasses and peered at the only person in the world he loved, the only person he couldn't afford to lose. Rhys had grown into a fine person, one any man would be proud to call his son.

"Is the McKenna woman worth the risk of involving yourself with Valerie Gleiter?"

Without hesitating so much as a beat, Rhys said, "She's worth it."

Realizing his hands were trembling, Jens made them into fists. "That Gleiter woman is dangerous to know. The men around her are falling like trees. Poor Fisk. And Magnus before him. Not that I ever liked or trusted Magnus...but his death was as mysterious as the rest of 'em, his body never being found and all."

"Tom Patterson wasn't connected to her."

"Not that you know. I've heard rumors."

"Anything specific?"

Jens shook his head. He didn't socialize, had merely overheard some gossip when he'd been forced to go into town for supplies a couple of months ago.

"Something to find out, then."

Rhys sounded so determined that Jens quaked inside. He couldn't lose the boy. Couldn't lose another person he loved. He would have to do something. He'd had his suspicions all along, since the second death months before. Now there were four and who knew how fast the count would rise. He'd left it alone, but maybe that had been a mistake. One he meant to correct.

Tonight.

AILEEN BROUGHT HER LAPTOP and recorder down to breakfast with her, and after eating, sat between the fireplace and Christmas tree in the common room to work. As she transcribed the interviews from the day before, she let sounds drift by her, paid them no mind as guests began checking in for the Christmas holiday. She actually felt soothed by the normalcy of activity around her. One woman asked for directions in the area, a couple simply wanted to check out cross-country skis. The buzz grew louder as a family chattered away about the different types of winter sports equipment available.

Aileen looked up just as the outside door opened again to admit Rhys Lindgren. Assuming he'd come to see her, she felt a little breathless.

Would he say something about their early-morning activities or had it all really been a dream?

"I'll be with you in a few minutes," a hassled-sounding Valerie told him. "As soon as I show these folks to the equipment shed." She indicated the family of four who'd been making so much chatter.

Rhys said, "I figured you might need some help with the extra guests coming in, and I'm available for work."

Valerie gave in to her surprise only for a moment before saying, "Come with me, then, and we can talk as soon as they have what they need."

Aileen stared openmouthed as the lodge owner led the way outside, the family followed and Rhys took up the rear. Just before he left the room, however, he zeroed in on her as if he'd known exactly where she was all the time. No smile of greeting lit his face. He seemed as serious as always.

What was that all about? Aileen wondered, her heart thudding. He didn't need the money. At least she didn't think he did. Even so, why would he want to work for Valerie Gleiter as a jack-of-all-trades? Why wouldn't he seek a job with the DNR or with some conservation group?

Multiplying questions ate at her, and it wasn't long before she realized she'd been staring at her laptop screen without adding a single line long enough that the battery had gone low. She shut down and was about to go back upstairs and hook the computer up to recharge when Valerie and Rhys returned.

"If you're serious about this, you'll need to bunk here," Valerie was saying. "You can go home on your days off, of course."

"No problem. I figure it's time I had a change of scenery. I can help with the guests and things you need done around here. I figure you could use me through the holiday rush, at least. Enough time for us both to decide if it's a relationship that works."

Valerie's expression turned speculative as she stared at Rhys, and Aileen was taken aback by the charge in the air she felt even from a distance. It was as if the lodge owner were sizing Rhys up for something other than his potential as an assistant. Something far more personal.

"Indeed. Sounds perfect," she said. "You have yourself a deal. I'll pay you what I was paying Fisk, and when the holiday rush dies down, we'll talk."

"Where do you want me to start?"

"A trip to town. We're low on food, so you need to stop at the market. I'll call in the order so you just have to pick it up. And the hardware store—Fisk ordered electrical and plumbing supplies last week, so they should be in."

"No problem. I'll get right on it."

Before he could get out the door, Aileen cheerily asked, "Mind if I hitch a ride? I was told that was part of the lodge's service."

She couldn't miss Valerie's annoyed expression even as Rhys said, "My pleasure," in a way that sent a flush of warmth through her, all the way to her toes.

"Give me a few minutes to go up to my room and get my jacket."

Rhys nodded. "I'll be out in the truck."

Once in her room, Aileen hooked up the computer to recharge. Then, before grabbing her jacket and scarf, she ran a brush through her hair and gloss over her lips. Her pulse was threading unevenly at the thought of being alone with Rhys again. She had to know the truth about what had happened to her in the night.

As she ran back down the stairs, she pulled on her jacket, and as an afterthought, patted her jeans pocket to make sure the protection pouch was still there. Even though she had no proof that anything supernatural was going on, she wasn't about to go anywhere without it.

To her surprise, Valerie stood alone behind the service counter. Considering how busy she'd been all morning, she deserved a break.

"Aileen, can I talk to you for a moment?"

"Sure."

"This is a little awkward…"

"What is it?"

"It's Rhys."

Had he left without her? Aileen took a quick look outside. His truck was there, and he was behind the wheel.

"I sense you like Rhys," Valerie said.

"I do." Aileen kept her answer nonchalant. She wasn't about to offer more.

"Now that he's working for me…and you're a guest…" Valerie sighed. "Well, a personal relationship doesn't seem appropriate, does it?"

The lodge owner was asking her not to see Rhys, and Aileen was pretty sure it didn't have anything to do with his being a new hire. Considering the way Valerie had sized him up earlier, added to their conversation about men the night before, Aileen figured the other woman was ripe for the picking. Rather, ripe to do the picking of a new man for herself.

"Perhaps you'd better speak to Rhys about that," Aileen said, trying to stay on a friendly level. "It seems…odd…that you would suggest to one of your guests what she could or could not do personally."

Valerie's gaze suddenly burned into her, and Aileen stepped back. The other woman was angry that she hadn't agreed. A little surprising, considering how well they'd gotten along the night before. She thought to say something to mollify Valerie and then changed her mind. It was the lodge owner who was inappropriate here.

Acknowledging that Valerie had for some reason decided she wanted Rhys for herself—which could be a bit uncomfortable as long as she stayed here—Aileen left the lodge and climbed into the truck without saying a word. The moment she buckled up, Rhys pulled away from the building.

Aileen took a big breath and tried to shake away the unsettled feeling. She was with Rhys, *wanted* to be with Rhys. So why couldn't she just appreciate the moment, revel in the sense of anticipation she'd felt before talking to Valerie? A charge shot between them, and she couldn't deny the anticipation she felt. For one, she wanted to know if they had been together last night or if it had really been a dream.

Before she could broach the subject, Rhys suddenly said, "I assume you're off for more interviews with the good citizens of Wolf Creek."

Not exactly what she wanted to hear from him, so she couldn't help the edge to her voice. "What if I am?"

"Then you have less sense than I gave you credit for."

Aileen clenched her jaw. First Valerie, now Rhys was giving her a hard time, both spoiling the romantic afterglow she'd been trying to hang onto.

"Ever since I got here, everyone keeps telling me what to do," she said. "Or what not to do."

"Look, it's not that I want to order you around, but I'm worried. I just want you to stay safe...lie low until things settle down in town. When you left me that message last night that you were followed..."

Aileen's irritation waned. She believed him. He simply was too blunt when he disapproved of something she did. When he went all alpha on her, he didn't have the social skills to make her warm up to his suggestions.

"I appreciate that," she said. "But I'm not a child. I've been taking care of myself for many years now." Not that she hadn't wondered what it would be like to have a man look after her needs.

Rhys pulled the truck over and put it in Park. They were at the edge of the property, yards from the paved road. Aileen felt her pulse pick up.

"We need to be straight with each other, Aileen. There's a real danger out there and I need to find answers. I can't do that if I'm isolated."

"Is that why you came looking for work at the lodge?"

"To learn the truth for myself, yes." He hesitated only a moment before adding, "And to make sure you were safe. You need my protection."

Aileen started. "You want to protect me? Why?"

"Because you're in danger. And because I have...feel...different when I'm with you."

Warmth flooded her. Coming from the wolf man, that awkward declaration was downright romantic.

"We have a connection that I can't explain," he added.

"I've felt it, too." Should she say something or not? "Last night, for instance." She chose her words carefully. "I had the feeling you were nearby."

"I wanted to make sure you were safe."

"You were there, then?" It really had happened?

"After getting your message, I spent the night on your deck so nothing could get to you."

Nothing rather than *no one.*

"And...that's it?" Then it had been a dream? She couldn't just come out and ask. Sighing, she said, "Actually, the reason I wanted to come out with you was to get your opinion about my scare last night."

"Go on."

"How about I show you?" she suggested. "You know the shortcut up ahead—the footpath into town?"

"Right."

"Find a place to park up there. We need to see the area in daylight."

Rhys started up the truck and turned onto the main road. A moment later, he pulled over again and parked. "So you came this way from town last night? In the dark? Why didn't you call for a ride back to the lodge?"

Aileen ignored his critical tone. She knew he was just worried for her.

"And have who pick me up?" she asked. "Fisk was dead, remember, and Valerie was taking care of things at the lodge." She took a big breath. "So back to my walk home…halfway back, I got the feeling I wasn't alone, that I was being followed. Then either my imagination was playing tricks on me or something actually hit me from behind and knocked me to my knees."

Rhys swore softly and gazed deep into her eyes. "That's all that happened to you?"

"I had a scare is all, but I wanted to come out here and see the tracks for myself." She stopped and pointed to a familiar-looking spot lined with bushes. The snow was messed up for several yards. "There. That's where I took the spill."

They walked to the area, where Rhys stooped and took a good look around. Aileen moved right past him and stopped suddenly, her breath caught in her throat.

"Animal tracks," she croaked, pointing them out. "Big enough to be made by a wolf."

Rhys was at her side in a moment. "They could also have been left by a large dog."

Not that he sounded convinced.

Aileen started walking, following the tracks back the way they'd come. "I heard footsteps. If it was a dog, it wasn't alone."

The tracks led through some bushes. On the other side, they disappeared.

"Just like they came from nowhere."

Rhys was stooping again. She came alongside him and crouched next to him. He was checking out a footprint made not by an animal, but by a boot with a circle and wave pattern cut into the sole. Aileen looked beyond him and swept her gaze along the trail of human footprints. No animal prints lay alongside them.

"The human prints stop here," she muttered.

"This pattern—have you ever seen it before?" Rhys indicated the circle and wave.

"I don't know. Maybe. Why?"

"Because I found prints like this around Tom Patterson's body and from that hunter who shot at us." He met her gaze. "And near Fisk Oeland's body."

A chill shot through her. "And here, where the animal tracks start where the footprints stop. What does it mean, Rhys?" she asked, thrusting her hand into her pocket to encircle the protection pouch. "Was Madam Sofia right when she warned me against a werewolf?"

Rhys stood and stared down at the tracks for a moment before saying, "We'd better get to town. I need to get those supplies for Valerie."

"No, wait!" She grabbed his arm and stopped him from moving off. "What's going on here, Rhys? What do you know?"

"Why do you assume I know anything you don't?"

"The pouch," she said, placing her hand on his chest. She could feel the lump under his jacket. "You got it from Madam Sofia, didn't you?" When he still didn't answer, she pulled her hand free from her pocket and held out her own protection pouch. "She gave this one to me."

Frowning, he met her gaze. "So you believe in werewolves?"

"I don't know what to believe…but I know there are forces beyond what the average person would consider normal. I know because my grandmother was a *bean feasa* and she passed her gifts to her grandchildren."

"What kind of gifts?"

"It's different for each of us. For me…dreams. I've both accepted and pretty much ignored them until recently. They're confusing…both real and not real. Hard to sort out. I had one early this morning."

"About a werewolf?"

Aileen's heart beat faster. She couldn't just blurt out that she'd seen him wearing the face of a wolf.

"About you…and me…together…"

Rhys's gaze deepened and he let out a sharp breath. Once more she felt her blood racing, every nerve in her body came alive. She swayed toward him.

"It was just a dream, right?" she asked.

His expression suddenly closed him off from her. "If that's what you need it to be."

She gaped at him. He really wasn't going to tell her? He turned his back on her and started back to the truck.

Apparently not.

"Let's get going," he said. "I don't want to be fired the same day I was hired."

What could she do but follow him?

The mood between them shifted and Aileen found herself pressed against the door as far away from Rhys as she could get. Why wouldn't he talk to her honestly about what he thought was going on? He didn't think his wolves had made a human kill—he'd made that very clear. And he was wearing the pouch, for heaven's sake.

Equally important was what might have

happened between them. Rhys had admitted he had feelings for her and wanted to protect her, so why couldn't he talk about what happened and reassure her?

Halfway to town, Rhys slowed the truck. "What's going on over there?"

Aileen looked to the right. Two men holding rifles and looking satisfied with themselves stood over a downed animal on the ground. An animal with streaky gray fur...

A wolf!

Recognizing Knute Oeland and Abe Hanson, Aileen felt her stomach knot. Before she could stop him, Rhys practically flew out of the truck.

Following, she yelled, "Rhys, wait!" What was to stop the men from turning their rifles on him?

Either Rhys didn't hear her or he was ignoring her. Either way, he was asking for trouble. That he was furious was obvious from his aggressive posture.

"What the hell do you think you're doing?" Rhys demanded.

"Getting justice for my brother Fisk," Knute said. "One down..."

His implication being this would be the first of a number of kills, Aileen thought wildly.

"I'll have the law down on you...murderer!" Rhys stepped forward threateningly.

Knute laughed. "Murder? No, that's what happened to Fisk. This is just a no-good predator. A damn wolf!" He spat on the dead animal. "And as far as I'm concerned, the only good wolf is a dead wolf!"

Rhys flew at him and knocked the rifle out of his hands. Knute reacted instantly, punching at Rhys with one fist, then the other. The men traded blows. Aileen's heart thundered at the damage they might cause one another. She didn't want to see Rhys end up in jail.

Her stomach knotted tighter when she looked over at Hanson, who wore an angry expression. In the end, while Knute might be wily, Rhys was faster than his opponent. He soon had him facedown in the snow, his knee in the wiry man's back, reminding Aileen of the way he'd subdued the disperser wolf.

"Another wolf killed," Rhys growled, "and I won't wait for the DNR or the feds to take care of you!"

"Get off him, Lindgren." Abe Hanson was looking like he needed to do something with his rifle. He was jiggling it nervously, bringing up the barrel.

"Don't!" Aileen pleaded.

She grabbed Rhys's jacket and tugged hard until he took the hint and got off Knute. The unpleasant man scrambled to his feet and retrieved his rifle.

"You're going to be sorry, Lindgren," Knute muttered, his white-coated front making him look like an angry snowman. Shifting his weapon in a threatening manner, he backed toward his truck. "C'mon, Hanson."

Abe Hanson didn't say anything, but his expression was belligerent as he turned to follow his friend. A moment later, they were in Knute's truck and driving away.

Rhys dropped to the ground next to the dead wolf, grief etched in his features as he stroked the pointed nose. "Faolan, old friend, rest in peace."

Tears sprang to Aileen's eyes. "Faolan?" The first wolf she'd seen.

Rhys didn't respond, just knelt there stroking the wolf's fur as if he could get a response. The intensity of his emotions was palpable, though. It wired off him in waves. She felt his anger-laced grief as if it were a tangible thing.

"We need to call the DNR," she said, pulling out her cell.

"I'll do it."

Standing, he took the phone from her and made the call.

"I doubt Oeland'll do any jail time," Rhys said, "not with what happened to his brother."

Aileen shivered as she remembered Rhys's threat to Knute should the man kill another wolf.

While they waited for the authorities to arrive, they stood there silently, holding hands and grieving for the loss of another innocent life.

VALERIE WAS BESIDE HERSELF by the time Rhys Lindgren's truck pulled up in front of the lodge. What had taken him so long? He'd been gone most of the day. The sun was already setting. Standing behind the desk, she watched Rhys alight. Even with dusk descending, she could see he was a fine figure of a man.

More than willing to let him take Fisk's place in ways other than as an employee, she wondered how long it would take to reel him in. Her hormones were already racing just thinking about it…

Aileen opened the passenger door and Rhys scrambled around to help her out. They stood and spoke for a moment. From the way he remained so close to her, seemed so concerned about her, it was obvious Rhys was smitten with the city woman.

Disturbed by the sight, Valerie snapped the pen she'd been holding. She'd forged a bond with Aileen and now her new friend was an obstacle Valerie would have to eliminate.

What would it take to drive the city woman away so she could have Rhys to herself?

She could see spending her life with *this* one. Finally a man who had it all—looks, intelligence, integrity. A man worthy of her. Surely having children with Rhys would be possible. And they would be magnificent.

When the couple entered, Valerie put on her game face. "That took longer than I expected. You can bring the truck around back, Rhys. There's a rear entry leading to the kitchen."

"The food...sorry, Valerie. We were sidetracked."

Valerie clenched and unclenched her jaw. "Excuse me?"

"We were with the authorities," Aileen explained. "On the way into town, we found Knute Oeland and Abe Hanson standing over a dead wolf."

"They killed it?"

"That surprises you?" Rhys asked. "Oeland has never tried hiding his hatred of wolves."

"But he's never actually killed one before, has he?"

"He's never lost a brother before," Aileen said. "His brand of justice. He indicated this was only the first. He'll undoubtedly try to kill every wolf he can find."

Valerie frowned. "Surely he'll be arrested."

"They're going to take him in for questioning when they find him," Rhys said. "Perhaps they will arrest him, but, as we were told, we didn't actually see him kill the wolf. Forensics will have to sort it out. And if they can't…"

Valerie wrapped her arms around her middle to ward away a sudden chill. "No wolf in the area will be safe until he's been stopped."

Valerie went through the motions of pretending to be calm. She told Rhys he could wait until tomorrow when he volunteered to go back into town to get the supplies. Then he and Aileen went to the dining room to eat. Luckily she had enough staff to take care of the meals without having to involve herself. She had to get out to think. Pulling on her jacket and gloves, she slipped outside.

No one could blame Knute for being upset about his brother's death, but he'd taken things into his own hands. Was threatening to kill other wolves. Not that she believed a wolf had killed Fisk.

Valerie was still freaked by her handyman's death. While she hadn't been in love with him, she hadn't wished him harm. And to die the way he had…

A horrible thought niggled at her. No matter that she tried to put it out of mind, she knew Magnus would have done as much to Fisk out of jealousy…

That thought went around and around in her mind all the way to her cabin, which was set far enough back to be out of sight from the lodge. She loved the place built into a hillside. She felt safe there. Usually...

Even before she got to the door, she knew that tonight, someone else was inside, and only one name came to mind.

Magnus...

She glanced up at the moon, a bare sliver away from being full.

What if the impossible had happened and her husband was still alive, after all?

Her first instinct was to run, but there would be no hiding from the man who should be dead.

Who *deserved* to be dead.

Blood rushing through her at an agonizing rate, Valerie crossed to the cabin door and threw it open.

Chapter Twelve

The wolf wanders closer and closer to town in search of Rhys.

Too close.

She tries to convince him to go back, to hide deep in the woods where he'll be safe.

Too late.

The men with rifles appear, but the wolf is used to being close to man and so doesn't run.

Too innocent.

Knute raises his rifle.

"No!" she screams as the bullet leaves the barrel and skims the air in slow motion and finds its target.

Aileen moaned and turned in bed, but fight as she would, she couldn't fully awaken from the nightmare. No use. The vision remained vivid in her mind. Knowing she had to see the rest, had to seek the truth, she let her eyes droop closed once more...

Faolan drops to his knees and bucks, tries to get back to his feet. Futile. He sinks to the ground and, with a whine that pierces her heart, goes still.

"No!" she cries again, flinging herself to her knees next to the animal.

Not Faolan but the black wolf of her childhood.

Under the full moon, she can see its wounds— open bleeding gashes. Life's blood flowing freely from myriad bites, it meets her gaze before its eyes slowly begin to close. She touches the blood-soaked fur, strokes the animal tenderly and feels the beat of its heart.

"Don't die!"

She sobs over its wounds, tears dropping from her eyes to mingle with the animal's blood. The wolf makes a soft sound and raises its head to lick her scraped hand. As its tongue laves the wounded flesh, a thrill shoots through her. And her blood—it pounds in a strange rush.

She can feel his pain like he's part of her.

"You'll be okay…just hang on…"

She chokes on the last words as she rises and looks around for a way out. Woods surround the clearing, and she realizes she is lost. But surely there will be a road somewhere nearby. And where there is a road, there are cars. And where there are cars, there would be people to help.

The wolf yelps and she knows it's her fault. If she had stayed in the tent like she was supposed to do, this wouldn't have happened.

"I'll save you like you saved me!" she promises.

Disoriented, she winds deeper and deeper into the woods, trees and bushes attacking but not stopping her. Exhausted, she pushes forward, visions of the fallen wolf filling her head. She can feel his pain, feel him grow weaker. He can't die because of her…he just can't!

It's dawn before she spots a lone car cutting through the woods and waves it down. An older couple fuss over her and the woman pulls her inside.

"Back that way!" she says as the car moves off. "The wolf is that way." She barely feels a thread of life still connecting her to him. "He needs our help!"

"It's you who needs help. John, we've got to get her to the emergency room."

"No! We've got to go back!"

She fights the woman and tries to get out the door, but the woman holds her in firm arms.

"Shush, now, shush. You could kill yourself jumping from a moving car."

No matter how she struggles, she can't free herself. The connection to the wolf flickers and dies. The car edges out of the woods. When it arrives in a big parking lot behind a bigger building, the woman helps her out of the car, but her legs won't work right.

And neither will her voice.

A doctor tries to make her talk, but she can't focus, can't answer his questions.

Her mind is a blank...

"Aw-woo-oo..."

Aileen sat straight up in bed, her heart pounding. The dream was bleeding into reality. She could still hear the wolves howl.

"Woo-ooo-woo..."

Still half-asleep, she climbed from her bed, slipped her feet into winter mules and made her way outside to the deck.

More wolf howls sent a shiver down to her toes, and she rubbed at her arms through her thick sweater to chase away the gooseflesh. She'd fallen asleep fully dressed.

"Aw-woo-oo..."

What was with the wolves? Was someone after them? Or were they mourning Faolan in their own fashion?

No sooner had she thought it than she spotted movement below. A human cutting across the frozen landscape. She leaned over the railing for a better look.

Rhys—where was he going?

"Rhys!" she called, but he didn't seem to hear her. He just kept moving toward the woods.

Instinct made Aileen pull on her boots and grab her jacket. She flew down the stairs and dressed for the outside and crossed the common room as quickly as she could. Even so, she feared she would be too late, that she wouldn't be able to pick up Rhys's trail.

After exiting the building, she headed the way she'd seen Rhys go. Drawn toward the eerie wolf howls that continued to split the night, she passed the equipment shed without stopping. She might be able to go faster on cross-country skis, but it would take some time to get equipment and put it on—if the shed was even open.

Head down, ears attuned to what now was a mournful chorus, she hurried through a stand of trees into the deep woods. There she pulled a flashlight from her pocket and swept the ground to find the trail Rhys made. Faster and faster she moved through the woods. No fear. No time to think about it. Rhys…Rhys was her only thought. She swore she could feel him. He was cold inside. Cold and hot all at once.

What did it mean?

Out of breath and with a stitch in her side, Aileen finally had to slow and stop for a moment. Gasping for air, she finally caught sight of him.

Ahead, Rhys stood dead still, his body stiff. He lifted his head as if he were sniffing the air. Then suddenly he was off, Aileen right behind him.

"Rhys, wait for me!"

He kept on and she had all she could do to keep from letting him outdistance her. Suddenly he shot out into a clearing. She followed and stopped dead at the sight before her.

Surrounded by the pack—howling wolves in a circle around him—Rhys stood over a dark bundle crumpled in the snow. Even from a distance, Aileen could tell it was a man.

With an anguished cry, Rhys dropped to his knees and howled along with the pack. The sound reverberated through her. And his raw emotion.

"Oh, no…"

Aileen's throat tightened as she guessed the identity of the dead man. Rhys had no relationship with anyone other than his father.

Jens Lindgren was dead.

And then something happened Aileen couldn't even imagine. Rhys's body shimmered and glowed with reflected moonlight. Her own nerves felt like live wires as he stretched and changed shape and then within a matter of seconds was no more. In Rhys's stead stood a black wolf, nose raised to the moon as it howled its grief.

Heart pounding, Aileen gaped at the sight.

So it was all true—the stories of creatures who were half wolf, half man. She could hardly breathe at the revelation. And at the niggling thought that Rhys could have been responsible for several deaths.

No, she couldn't believe it. Wouldn't.

Murder wasn't in Rhys or he would have avenged Faolan by killing Knute Oeland and Abe Hanson on the spot. His having anything to do with the recent deaths was unthinkable. He was a good and kind man.

When he was a man...

Aileen took tentative steps toward the black wolf...toward the pack...toward the body...

The black wolf sensed her presence and turned to face her. She looked into his eyes...familiar eyes...and her breath simply stopped for a moment. She'd seen those eyes just a short time ago...in her dream. This was the black wolf from her dream!

Was it possible?

She was beginning to think anything was possible—even her befriending a pack of wolves. They looked her way, but didn't react. Walking through the perimeter they'd set up straight to the black wolf, stopping yards from the others, she felt no fear. Not until she took a better look at the body of Jens Lindgren, throat ripped out, his head lolling, his neck apparently snapped by powerful jaws. Her stomach churned and she had to look away to control her reaction.

The wolves once more began to howl. For their dead friend. For Rhys's father.

These wolves hadn't done the deed.

Then who?

The mournful sounds pierced her soul, and without thinking, Aileen knelt next to the black wolf and put her arms around his neck. Her tears streaked his fur and her blood began to thunder in her veins. Grief like she had never felt before filled her, crowded out her calm. She was feeling what the wolf was feeling. The connection was real and strong and had lasted for nearly two decades. Would last between them forever, if he would let it.

Gradually, she felt a shift that whipped through her body and she realized that Rhys was back. They stared at each other for several minutes before he finally said, "I need to call the authorities."

A short while later, the area was lit with battery-generated lights. There was a confusion of footprints, both wolf and human. The circle and wave pattern showed up again, leading away from the body, as if the creature that had killed Jens had changed back to a man and walked away. Not that Aileen dared say a word, and if Rhys noticed, he was keeping the information to himself, as well.

As the coroner examined the body, Sheriff Caine himself took their statements.

After which he said, "Look, as much as I would like to stop the violence against your wolves before it starts, I don't see that's going to happen this time. First Oeland, now your father." He shook his head. "Now we'll be lucky if we can keep anything under control."

"No normal wolf did this," Rhys said.

"So you think the creature is sick."

Rhys hesitated only for a second. "Absolutely. It wasn't my...our pack. I can account for them all. They were all here. You heard their howls."

"That doesn't mean one of them didn't kill your father."

"You obviously don't understand the nature of wolves or you would know that wouldn't happen."

"Please, Sheriff," Aileen said. Why couldn't he just back off for a minute?

Caine looked at her squarely in the eye as if taking her measure. "I don't even know why you're here, missy, sticking your nose where it doesn't belong." Then to her surprise, he said, "The two of you can go."

Rhys shook his head. "My father—"

"Won't be released for a day or two until the coroner is done with him."

Jens's body was already being prepared for transport. Rhys couldn't seem to take his eyes from the scene.

Aileen tugged at his arm. "C'mon," she said softly. "There's nothing more we can do here now."

For once Rhys let her take the lead. As they walked away from the kill site, she glanced down and nearly froze when she saw the print left by Sheriff Caine's boot—a circle and wave pattern. Her heart began to thud and Rhys glanced at her questioningly.

She couldn't tell him. Not here. He might go off on the sheriff and the print might mean nothing.

Rhys's cabin was closer than the lodge, so Aileen asked one of the deputies for a ride. She held Rhys's hand in a tight grip all the way there.

When they got inside, she said, "I could stand a drink." Her hands were shaking and a chill was shooting through her that she couldn't control. Two bodies and counting. She hoped to God she wouldn't have to see a third.

Though he didn't say anything, Rhys nodded and headed for a cabinet. Opening it, he took out a bottle and two glasses. After filling them, he handed her one. Though she didn't even like the taste of whiskey, Aileen downed the liquor in one gulp.

Then, unable to hide from the truth any longer, she asked, "What are you, Rhys?"

He finished his drink and shook his head. But he gazed straight into her eyes when he said, "I'm not sure."

"How is that possible?"

"My memories before being here are vague, more like dreams than reality. Maybe they were just dreams. What I remember is my life slipping away. There was a girl…" He gazed at her intently and again she was aware of his so, so familiar amber eyes. "*You*…and then Jens found me and brought me here. He doctored me, gave me a life when I couldn't remember any other one. He called me his son and taught me everything I know," Rhys said, his voice breaking slightly. "I was the son of his heart as he was my father. What am I going to do without him?"

He was devastated. She could see the grief etched in his features. Unable to stop herself, she moved to him and put her arms around him.

Realizing her dream and the wolf attack on him were one and the same, not certain of what it meant—her grandmother's gift sent her dreams, but they were always so mixed up that she had to somehow make sense of them—Aileen decided figuring it all out could wait. Rhys couldn't. At the moment he was a shell of himself, without focus, without substance and she couldn't stand to see him this way.

"I'm not Jens, but I'm here for you," she said, brushing her lips across his. "You have me. Let me help you." She cradled his face with both hands and kissed him again, her mouth lingering over his a moment.

Rhys seemed to rouse himself from some waking slumber. He deepened the kiss and encircling her with his arms, pulled her tightly against him as if he meant to keep her there forever. His heartbeat called to hers and they joined in rapid union, beating as one. She felt as if she was leaving her own body to inhabit something foreign and wonderful and scary.

Rubbing his back, she said, "It's late. You should try to get some sleep."

"I can't sleep."

"Then rest. You're not a machine. You can't just keep going."

He led her to his room and pulled her into the bed with him. It was a sleigh bed layered with down, an afghan carelessly tossed across the foot. Pulling the afghan over them, she curled against his side and rested her head in the hollow at his shoulder. Her very presence seemed to comfort him, and eventually he relaxed against her.

Why didn't it bother her, knowing Rhys wasn't like other men? Even if he was more than human, he wasn't evil. She knew that in her very soul. The way she'd known the first time they'd met, when he'd saved her from certain death, that they were one, meant to be.

There was no other explanation—he was the black wolf of her dreams.

Now she simply had to figure out what that meant.

RHYS DIDN'T SLEEP.

He stayed in bed and watched Aileen, was aware of her every movement, her every sigh as she settled in to slumber. Being close to the woman he loved had given him only temporary respite from his grief and growing anger.

You have me...let me help you...

Her words rolled through his mind. Did he really have her? Even if she was willing, how could he let her sacrifice herself for him?

When her eyes opened, his heart thudded. He could lose himself in those eyes. He could lose himself in her. She reached out and her touch was electric. Every nerve was on fire for her. He didn't know anything but wanting her. For a short while, he could forget about Father, about his need for justice and take solace in what she offered.

He trailed his hand from her full breast, down her flat belly to the valley between her thighs. She pressed into his hand, moaned as he pressed back. It gave him pleasure to watch her as he rubbed her through the cloth...more pleasure to feel her as he dipped his hand under her waistband and down to the pooled wetness that was just for him.

Her heart was beating so fast...he could hear it...and the next thing he knew his was beating in unison.

He was hard and wanted nothing more than to take her right then, but he kept himself in check as her breathing deepened and she grew restless and tilted her hips for him.

"Rhys," she murmured, pulling her sweater up over her head, the lace cups of her bra below her breasts so that they were fully exposed to him.

Her nipples had already stiffened in response to his intimate touch. He stretched out with her and suckled one and then the other. She tried to tug at him, to pull him on top of her, but he wouldn't let up working her, not until she lost control and cried out. Then he kissed her and loosened his pants and freed himself so he could take her.

She was ready for him, tilting her hips and grasping him like a fist. He shuddered as he sank into her and began to stroke her while watching her changing expressions. His head went light and sensation swamped him. He took her to the brink and pulled back, then kissed her to still any protest.

Rolling her over and with an arm slid under her at the waist, he pulled her up to her knees, leaving her body open to him. Then he entered her from behind and stroked her inside with the same rhythm as he did her outside with his hands. He slid in all the way and then nearly pulled free of her. At her cry of protest, he repeated the movement over and over, faster and faster until he felt the inner explosion that bound them together.

For a moment, the universe shifted and they were fully connected, their hearts beating in tandem. He sensed her every want, her every need, heard her every thought—*I love you!*—felt her every emotion.

They were one...

But nothing that perfect lasted. As they lay together, him spooned behind her, and she drifted off, that sense of oneness dissipated and he felt isolated once more.

And the image that would always be burned into his mind like a permanent photograph—Father with his jugular ripped open, shock etched permanently on his face—haunted him.

Sitting up, Rhys pulled a plastic bag from the bedside drawer and held it out in the moonlight shafting through the bedroom windows. He was so intent on studying the contents that he didn't know Aileen had stirred until he felt her pressed against his back, her chin hooked over his shoulder.

"What is that?" Her breath feathered his ear, making his insides tighten in response.

"Part of a cigarette."

"I can see that. I mean what's the significance?"

"It could be a clue. If the saliva matches the saliva on Fisk's throat…" He sighed. "The trick is to get the test done without raising suspicions."

"Maybe I can help." She took the plastic bag from him and set it on the other nightstand. "In the meantime, you need to sleep."

Rhys didn't argue. He stretched out alongside her. This felt so natural, so right. He couldn't help but want Aileen…couldn't help wanting a future with her. He'd been aware that part of him had been missing all these years. She was the piece that made the puzzle whole.

That made him whole.

If only she could change him, take away the uncertainty. The nightmares.

How could he ask her to share his private hell when he wasn't even sure of his own actions in the past? Of what he might do in the future?

Of one thing he was certain—if it was the last thing he ever did, he would find Father's killer and make sure the bastard got the justice he deserved.

If he had to take the law into his own hands... he couldn't let her be part of that.

Chapter Thirteen

By the time they got back to the lodge late the following morning, Donovan was there for some reason, pacing the length of the common room.

"Where the hell have you been, Aileen?" he demanded, all the while glaring at Rhys. "Are you trying to scare years off my life or what?"

Aileen glanced from her brother to the man she loved, who was staring back equally intent— two alpha males struggling for domination. For a moment amused, she looked back and forth between them, but when it seemed that they wouldn't let up without intervention, she stepped closer to Rhys and glared at Donovan.

"Rhys, the man without manners is my brother, Donovan Wilde. Donovan, this is Rhys Lindgren. As to your question, I couldn't leave Rhys alone after his father was killed. I'm sure that's why you're here, to get the facts. Right?"

Gaze still locked with Rhys's, Donovan said, "I'm here to take you home with me."

Irritated at her brother's high-handedness, she asked, "What makes you think I would leave?"

Finally, Donovan looked at her. "You're not safe here."

"No one is safe here—"

"He's right, Aileen," Rhys said, his tone filled with concern. "You should go with him."

"What?" Her stomach knotted.

"Your brother wants to protect you."

"I thought *you* wanted to protect me."

"Apparently I can't. Father is dead. I don't want you to be next. Go with him, Aileen."

"I'm not going anywhere."

She couldn't believe he wished her away after all they'd gone through together. After the closeness they'd shared through the long night.

"I have to take care of some things," Rhys said. "I can't be with you all the time."

"Then, go." Aileen's stomach churned. "Do what you have to do."

Rhys hesitated only a moment before nodding and turning his back on them. She watched him make his way to his truck. Not once did he look back.

Not once had he opened up and expressed any feelings for her, either. She might think he didn't have any if they didn't have such a strong connection. That meant he was fighting it. Trying to drive her away for her own good, of course. Thickheaded male that he was.

He didn't understand what it meant to be a McKenna. To have a legacy to live up to.

Act selflessly in another's behalf...

She would, if it was the last thing she ever did.

Swallowing her momentary disappointment, she turned to her brother. "You should go, too."

"Not until we talk this through."

Aileen spotted another vehicle pulling up outside. A family piled out of a van and started hauling out suitcases and large packages decorated with Christmas wrapping and big bows. And Valerie came out of her office. No privacy here anymore. The last thing she wanted was to face questions about why Rhys wasn't around. If the owner didn't already know.

Sighing, she said, "Fine. Let's get away from here. Go up to my room." She led her brother away from the incoming chaos.

Once inside her room, she threw her jacket on the bed, but she couldn't settle down, so she opened the door to the deck and stepped outside. The day was warmer than it had been since she'd arrived, and the sun was shining as if there were something to be grateful for.

Donovan was right behind her, saying, "So tell me what's really going on."

"It's complicated."

"Aileen—"

"All right."

If she could tell anyone the truth—or at least her version of it—that would be Donovan. Donovan was as much a part of the McKenna legacy as she was—he could connect to his wolves, see through their eyes—so he was all-too-familiar with things that weren't considered normal. Taking into account the investigation going on, they could use his help. Considering wolves would die if this situation weren't otherwise resolved, he would want to help.

"I assume you've heard the rumors," she began.

"About wolves attacking the victims. Yes."

"About werewolves."

"What? Oh, come on. People around here don't really believe that nonsense, do they?"

Images of Fisk's and Jens's lifeless, bloodied bodies flashed through her mind.

"I believe it. I wish it were nonsense." She looked her brother square in the eye. "You seem shocked. You don't believe me after what you've experienced?"

"Convince me."

Aileen told him everything from Madam

Sofia's warning her first day in town to their finding the footprints that turned to animal prints where she'd been followed. She stopped and looked away before she revealed Rhys's secret.

"What else?"

"Isn't that enough?" She focused on a path in the distance that led deep into the forest.

"I know you, Aileen. Ever since you were a kid I could read you when you were trying to hide something. You can't meet my eyes."

Hearing the worry in his voice, she said, "Don't press it, okay?"

"It's him. Rhys. Right? Are you trying not to tell me he's a werewolf?"

Aileen sighed and faced him. If she didn't tell someone… "I'm not sure what Rhys is exactly. Werehuman, maybe."

"Huh?"

"Remember the day I got lost in the woods? I do now. I remember."

"How? It just came back to you?"

"A little at a time. Through dreams," she clarified. "You know that's my legacy."

"I thought you didn't believe in Gran's gifts."

"I didn't want to pursue mine. That's different than not believing. As a kid, I wanted to fit in, so I chose to be disinterested in what I couldn't explain. To what others wouldn't understand. I can't be indifferent anymore. I needed answers and I went after them. It's why I came here, Donovan. To find myself. And now I have." She took a big breath. "I'm convinced I met Rhys that night I went missing…that he saved my life."

"How?"

"I was attacked."

"By a wolf?"

"By a werewolf."

Her brother snorted. "What did he do? Shoot it with a silver bullet?"

"Joking about it is beneath you, Donovan!" She struggled to keep her emotions under control. "What if someone laughed at you?"

He immediately sobered. "You're right. Sorry. So what did happen?"

"They fought and he won. The creature ran off."

"So he had what? A knife?"

"Teeth. He wasn't in human form."

The change in Donovan's expression was startling. It was suddenly intent and scary. If he wasn't her brother, she might be nervous. "What the hell! Then you *are* telling me he's a werewolf."

"I think…I think he was a wolf, Donovan. And when he was attacked…"

"He turned into a human?"

She nodded. "I know it sounds crazy, but is it any crazier than a man turning into a wolf? He fought to save me and was badly wounded. I thought he was going to die. I told him I wouldn't let him, that I would save him. I went off in search of help. I couldn't find the campsite. I couldn't find the road for hours. Then I saw a car and flagged it down—"

"The old couple who brought you to the E.R."

"I tried to tell them." Remembering clearly now, she felt her eyes sting with unshed tears. "I tried to make them go back, but they wouldn't. The wolf and I had a connection and somehow I felt his life slipping away…and I thought he'd died…and then I just…" She swiped at her eyes. "Well, I was responsible and remembering was too much to bear…"

Donovan wrapped his arms around her and kissed the top of her head. "The woman said you were babbling some nonsense about a wolf when they found you."

"You never told me."

"Dad and Skelly and I thought you'd had a terrible scare and that bringing it up would be the worst thing we could do. I'm sorry if we made the wrong choice."

"You did what you thought was right for me at the time. I wasn't ready to remember." She pulled out of his arms and tried to reassure him. "What could I have done with that knowledge at eleven?"

Donovan nodded. "So you and Rhys Lindgren?"

"I felt the connection the first time I met him. And every time. I love him, Donovan, and I always will. I've loved him for twenty-two years. You have to accept that. He's a good being, no matter if he's exactly like us or not. We'll find a way to work it out. In the meantime, you have to help us."

"Help you with what?"

"For one, with this." From her pocket, she pulled the plastic bag holding the cigarette butt. "Rhys found it at Fisk Oeland's death site. We need to know about the saliva, if it matches what they find on Fisk and Jens."

"And if it's a match, what am I supposed to do with that information?"

"I don't know yet." She looked away from him again. Her gut told her Rhys wouldn't leave it alone until the killer was stopped, one way or the other. "What kind of justice is there for a creature people believe exists only in the movies? But we need to know first."

"One of the lab guys owes me a favor." He took the bag and stuck it in his pocket. "I'll do it."

"Thank you. With all the tests they're probably doing, there might be more. You work for the DNR. You have influence. If it comes down to it, you need to help me protect Rhys. That's what you do for the people you love, right? You protect each other."

"You're sure he's the one Gran wished for you."

It wasn't a question. He'd already accepted it. "He's the one."

"I don't have to like it, but I trust your judgment. I'll do whatever I can to help."

"That's all I can ask." She gave her big brother a hug and shivered. "It's cold. What are we doing out here, anyway?"

They went inside and down to the dining room where Donovan had a big lunch and Aileen forced herself to eat something. She needed to keep up her strength if she was going to be of any use to Rhys.

What was he doing? She tried calling twice, but both times reached his voice mail, both times asked him to call her as soon as he heard her message.

"Maybe he's tied up making arrangements for the funeral," Donovan said.

"He doesn't know when they'll release Jens's body. I need to find him. Can I hitch a ride into town with you?"

"If that's what you need to do." Donovan took one look at her determined expression and nodded. "But if anything weird happens, if you learn anything you didn't know before, I want you to call me."

"Fine."

Aileen signed the food bill to her account and they left. Donovan stopped in the men's room and she headed out for the truck as Valerie was greeting another set of newcomers—a couple with two little kids and a teenager.

"Just go right in," Valerie said. "I'm right behind you." She picked up several bags and, spotting Aileen, asked, "Has your boyfriend forgotten to tell me he quit the job I just gave him?"

"You haven't heard? His father was killed last night."

Valerie fumbled with the bags and cursed under her breath as they went flying out of her hands. She quickly started gathering them back together. "I—I need to get inside."

Aileen bent to get one of the smaller bags that had gotten away from Valerie. As she made to stand, she noticed the imprint in the snow—a circle and wave pattern. Blinking, she stood and said, "Nice boots. Where did you find those?"

"These old things?" Taking the errant bag, Valerie glanced down at them and frowned.

"Canada. Some trip or other I made with Magnus."

Then she rushed inside, leaving Aileen in thought so deep that she didn't even realize her brother was standing there waiting for her.

"Are you coming or what?"

"Huh? Yeah." Aileen climbed in the truck.

Canada. Madam Sofia had thought the werewolf had migrated along with wolves from Canada. And Sheriff Caine had gone north on a fishing trip with Valerie and her late husband. He had boots that left the same imprint.

A fact that she'd forgotten to mention to Rhys.

RHYS FINISHED MAKING THE funeral arrangements dependent on the release of the body. After which he paid a visit to the sheriff's office and insisted on seeing Caine himself. The man sat with his feet up on his desk, his attention on the television across the room. Caine was watching a football game.

"I want an update on my father's death," Rhys demanded, having to raise his voice over audience cheers when someone made a touchdown.

Caine muted the sound. "What's to update? You know what happened as well as I do."

"I'm talking about the investigation. What are your men doing?"

"What's there to do? Look, Lindgren, I know you're fond of those wolves and all—"

"You're ignoring the human element."

Caine's visage went dark. "Your father wasn't killed by a man."

"Nor by a wolf," Rhys argued.

"What else is there?"

"You tell me, Sheriff."

Caine appeared taken aback for a moment, then said, "If it looks like a duck and quacks like a duck…"

"Do ducks wear winter boots? Or do wolves?"

That took the wind out of him for a moment. Then he asked. "What the hell are you talking about?"

"The same prints keep showing up at the kill sites—Patterson's, Oeland's and now my father's." He deliberately looked at the soles of Caine's boots. "Or have you managed to ignore that information?"

The sheriff dropped his feet to the floor. "I can't acknowledge information that I don't have."

"Well, you have it now. The print consists of a circle and waves. Sound familiar?"

Caine sat back against his chair and shook his head. "Grief does weird things to a person. You got someone to talk to? Maybe that McKenna woman? I would let her comfort you if I were you."

Rhys balled his hands into fists so that he didn't jump the bastard. So Caine wasn't going to answer. Wasn't going to admit that his boots had made the imprint Rhys had described.

"No accounting what grief can do to a person, all right," Rhys said. "Especially when an investigation is being curtailed by the powers that be. Sometimes one simply has to take a personal interest in seeing that justice comes to those who deserve it."

"Don't be a fool, Lindgren." Caine's eyes blazed at him. "Don't take the law into your own hands."

"Warning noted."

With that, Rhys left the sheriff's office, feeling the man's stare pierce his back like a knife. He drove straight to his cabin faster than he should, but a four-wheeled vehicle couldn't help him shake his emotions, so when he parked the truck, he got out and first walked, then jogged into the forest where the late afternoon stretched out the shadows as the sun sank low in the western sky.

Suddenly he had so many emotions for the only two people he'd ever loved that he didn't know what to do with them.

His jog became a flat-out run, and then he did something he'd never before done in daylight. In an effort to work off his charged emotions, he pictured himself stretched out, long black legs eating the trail and suddenly heat shot through him—and the pain, the agonizing pain—and suddenly he was there.

He was conscious now. Ever since his last visit with Madam Sofia, he wore the pouch and was able to keep his awareness intact. When he transformed once more, he would remember everything that happened.

As he ran, his love for Aileen burned like a flame inside him. No matter that he'd tried to chase her away. That had been for her good, not his. He wouldn't put her in danger in the short term…and in the long term…well, there was no possibility of a long-term relationship.

As he ran, he was so intent on the woman he loved, that he became careless, didn't see the men until it was too late.

As he ran, a shot rang out, crashing through the trees toward him.

He tried to turn.

Thump…

Pain bloomed in his side. His legs buckled. He fought, but his sight grew dim and as he fell to the snow-covered earth, it felt like an icy-cold grave.

Chapter Fourteen

Donovan had let her off at the funeral parlor where Aileen learned she had missed Rhys by more than an hour. She never should have had lunch with Donovan. The afternoon was already half gone. Out on the street again, she looked around, but saw no sign of Rhys. Where the heck could he have gone?

She tried his cell. Voice mail. His home phone. Voice mail.

Surely he wasn't trying to shut her out. Or was he? Now what? Before going back to the lodge, she decided to check the Cozy Café. If he wasn't in there, maybe Liz could tell her where to look.

Another dead end.

She got a cup of coffee and sat near a window for half an hour, hoping he might go by. A waste of her time. More calls. More frustration.

She might as well go back to the lodge before

dark. This was the winter solstice. Tonight would be the longest night of the year and it was coming on them fast.

"If you see Rhys, tell him I'm looking for him, would you?" she asked Liz.

"Sure thing, hon. Men aren't like us women when it comes to grieving. He probably just needs some time to himself, you know?"

"I know." Aileen gave the woman the best she could in the way of a smile and left the diner.

She'd barely touched toe to the sidewalk when a man nearly knocked her over as he rushed by.

"What's the hurry?" she muttered.

Other people were hurrying, as well.

She looked down the street to see a couple dozen gathering around a truck parked in front of the Oak Leaf Tavern. They seemed agitated and their voices were raised.

Did it have something to do with Jens's death?

Hurrying toward the growing, angry crowd, Aileen got a sick feeling. And when she heard the words *black wolf* shouted, panic twisted her insides. She ran flat-out, then pushed her way through the crowd.

"How do I know I won't be next?" a woman asked.

"It only kills men," another answered as Aileen broke through to the center. "And right now it ain't gonna do nothin' to no one. Harry used a tranquilizer dart to bring it down."

The wolf was collared and chained and having trouble staying on its feet as if it was trying to pull itself out of its drugged stupor. No doubt in Aileen's mind—this was Rhys in wolf form. She felt his pain and confusion. Madam Sofia claimed a werewolf could turn at will. What in the world had possessed Rhys to change into a wolf now?

A man she didn't know carried out what looked like a dog cage and set it down in the street. A second man poked the wolf with a stick to get him to move to the cage. He poked again, and the wolf cried out.

Aileen tried not to be sick. "Stop that!" she cried. "You don't have to hurt him."

"Hurt isn't good enough," another man in the crowd muttered. "Jens Lindgren trusted them critters and look what happened to him."

She wasn't about to argue the fact now. It wouldn't do any good. "Call the DNR to take care of the wolf." Not the best solution, but a delaying tactic, and perhaps the only one that would leave Rhys alive.

"We don't need no one to tell us what to do with a killer!" came a familiar voice.

The crowd parted, leaving an opening for Knute Oeland.

Aileen saw the axe in his hand as he pulled it back behind his head, obviously about to throw it at the wolf. Suddenly Knute went flying and the axe fell harmlessly to the ground.

"Enough, Oeland!" Sheriff Caine ordered. "I don't want trouble from the feds. Go home." He looked around at the people in the crowd, some of whom were dispersing. His gaze stopped at Aileen. "All of you. Now!"

A yelp brought her attention back to the guy with the stick. Another poke and the wolf stumbled into the cage. The man slammed the door and set the lock, asking, "What do we do with him now, Sheriff?"

Caine indicated the building on the other side of the truck. Oak Leaf Tavern. "You have a storeroom in back, right?"

"Yeah. So?"

"Let's get it in there until we can get someone from the DNR to come and take care of it."

As Aileen watched, the two men lifted the cage and carried it around back. The wolf was lying on his side, making her hope he wasn't hurt.

What to do?

She thought about calling Donovan, having him come back to claim the wolf as a representative of the DNR. Then he could bring Rhys back to the cabin and release him and she would stay nearby until he took human form again.

Though she fingered the cell in her pocket, she couldn't bring herself to do it. She didn't want to get her brother in trouble, and if the wrong people found he'd claimed the wolf under the guise of the DNR only to release him, Donovan could lose his job.

She would have to do it herself…but how?

Suddenly she realized Sheriff Caine was standing over her. "My advice to you, missy, is to get yourself back where you came from. You don't belong here. You could've gotten yourself hurt real bad today by interfering. The folks around here don't truck with losing their own. They won't take kindly to you telling them they're wrong."

"I'll try to stay out of trouble."

"That mean you're not leaving?"

"Pretty much."

"Don't say I didn't warn you."

She watched him walk away. Her gaze dropped to the ground and the imprint left by the soles of his shoes. If he was the werewolf, then what was his game here? Perhaps it was all a charade, a way to protect himself from discovery.

Thankfully, the sun was setting. Working under cover of darkness would be an advantage. Maybe she could get into the tavern through a back door or window and free the wolf before anyone knew she was there.

Stalling for time, Aileen strolled along Main Street, peered into windows, stopped to use a restroom, bought a cup of hot chocolate in a disposable cup that she could carry out on the street and drink to warm up inside.

Finally, it was dark enough.

She walked past the tavern, then when she was sure no one was watching, ducked between buildings and headed for the back. The place had both a delivery door and a normal back door. Both were locked. She looked through the grilled window into a dark room. She sensed movement. Emotion. *Rhys.*

Praying no one would spot her, she flicked on her flashlight and scanned the room, stopping when something glowed back at her. Two somethings. The eyes of the wolf. He was staring at her as if pleading for help.

She stared back for a moment and wondered since he was alone why he didn't try transforming. As a human, he could manage to open the lock himself. Then she took a better look at the cage. A dog cage might be big enough to contain a wolf, but it was too small for a human. Rhys simply wouldn't fit.

Which meant she had to get in the storeroom

to free him. Running her light through the window over the locking mechanism, she realized it was blocked by the nature of the grill—no room for her to get her fingers inside to unfasten the lock even if she broke the glass.

If she couldn't get into the storeroom from the outside, she would have to do it from inside—from the tavern itself. Checking her jacket pocket, she was relieved to feel her tape recorder. She could use wanting interviews for her thesis as a cover story.

A woman with a plan, Aileen slipped between buildings and around to the front door of the Oak Leaf. Certain no one saw her furtive movements, she tried to relax as she entered. Her outer show of confidence was more bravado than anything else. Her insides knotted and her knees felt like jelly. Still, she hid her fear as best she could.

As she walked right up to the bar, she glanced around to see a handful of customers, mostly men, mostly around the pool table at the opposite end. Knute Oeland and Abe Hanson were among them.

Damn! Just her luck.

Aileen turned to the bartender, a young guy with longish hair, a handlebar mustache and a name tag that identified him as Dave. "Coffee with a little something to keep me warm."

Not that she wanted alcohol—she needed a

clear head—but this was a bar and she wasn't about to raise suspicions by not ordering.

"Something to keep you warm? What's that? This is Wisconsin, the home of the brewski."

"And here I thought this state was famous for cheese."

"Just pullin' your leg, darlin'—one toe warmer comin' up."

As Aileen set out a ten to pay for the drink, a short, dark-haired woman wearing an Oak Leaf apron stopped right next to her. "Knute's buying another round for the boys."

"You got it, Cherry."

"That's *Cheryl*," the woman muttered as the bartender handed Aileen her spiked coffee and change. And after he turned to fill the waitress's order, Cheryl made a face at Aileen. "Like he can't remember my name."

"I think Dave likes to keep things light."

"Yeah." The waitress rolled her eyes. "You're new."

"I've only been in town a few days."

"You that biology student with the big interest in wolves?"

"That would be me."

Aileen looked over the waitress's shoulder to the pool table. She didn't think Knute had spotted her yet.

Cheryl looked, too, and her expression was serious when she said, "You might not want to be here tonight."

A thrill shot through Aileen at the warning. "I came to interview people for my thesis." She pulled out her tape recorder and set it on the bar as if to prove it.

"With another man killed, his throat ripped out?"

"I'm trying to be fair, to see all sides."

"Maybe you ought to try somewhere else," Cheryl suggested. "Those guys can be trouble, especially after they've had a couple of beers."

"Thanks for the heads-up."

The bartender slid her tray toward the waitress. Cheryl shrugged at Aileen. "Good luck," she said, before hauling the beers across the room to the men who already seemed to have had one too many.

"She's got a point, you know," Dave said. "Tonight's not a good night. Maybe you ought to put that away"—he indicated the tape recorder—"and try another day."

"Okay, I can take a hint."

Aileen made a show of reluctance as she put the tape recorder back in her pocket. Not that she was about to go anywhere without Rhys.

Act selflessly in another's behalf...

"But before I take that long, cold walk back to the lodge," she said, "I could use a restroom."

"Back that way." Dave aimed a thumb at a doorway that led to the back of the building.

"Thanks."

Leaving him two singles, Aileen pocketed the rest of her change, then left her coffee cup untouched and headed in the direction of the restroom.

Once through the doorway into the hall, however, she took a quick glance over her shoulder. No one currently in the bar could see where she was headed. Hopefully, neither Knute nor Abe had noticed her at all. Taking a big pulse-calming breath, she passed up the facilities and kept going toward a set of doors in back.

She pressed her ear to the first, and when she didn't hear any voices inside, carefully opened it only to have something pop out at her and send her stomach spinning. The mop hit the doorjamb with a loud thunk, but before it could fall to the floor, she caught it and set it back inside the janitor's closet.

Pulse racing, she froze for a moment and listened hard. If anyone in the bar had heard, she couldn't tell. The buzz from voices didn't change and above them, she caught the sharp click of a cue stick hitting a ball.

Her hand trembled as it wrapped around the knob of the second door that opened to darkness. Light from the hall illuminated a nearby case of beer. This was it, then. Slipping inside, she pulled her flashlight from a pocket and snapped it on.

The wolf was on his feet and he was staring at her.

"It's going to be all right. Just give me a minute."

Though she didn't know if Rhys was cognizant, she figured a low, soothing tone would ease the wolf's nerves.

"I'm going to have you out of here in no time."

First thing, she needed to unlock the window and open it before approaching the cage. There were two locks. She twisted the first open and flipped the second to the side.

The wolf watched her every movement. Its growing excitement built in her, too.

"Just let me get this window…"

The window was old and big and heavy and made a sound of protest that set her heart to racing. At last, it was open all the way.

She watched the wolf as she approached the cage. "Rhys, it's me, Aileen. If you're in there, if you can hear me, you have to get away fast through the window."

Her hands shook as she unbolted the cage door's lock. Suddenly the storeroom door flew open and the light went on.

"Go, now!" she cried, swinging open the cage door.

"I told you she was up to no good!"

Knute's voice jolted through her. Halfway out of the cage, the wolf turned and with a deep growl, bared its teeth.

"Go!" Aileen yelled. *Before it's too late.*

"Someone get a gun!"

The wolf wasn't going anywhere, so a frantic Aileen pushed at him. "Now!"

The touch seemed to spread the sense of urgency. The wolf's muscles bunched and with one leap, he surged through the open window.

"Here's a rifle."

Knute took the weapon and made for the window, but Aileen stepped in his way and put her hands on the barrel, shoving it up toward the ceiling. "You'll have to shoot me first."

"That can be arranged."

"Knute, don't do anything crazy," Abe said.

"Me? It's this bleeding heart who's crazy. She just set a killer free."

Aileen argued, "That wolf didn't kill anyone!"

"You can't know that for sure."

"And you can't know that he did."

"Bitch!" Knute spat, shoving her against the window so that it rattled like it might shatter.

Quaking inside, Aileen tried to get out, but

Knute wouldn't let her past him. "Oh, no you don't," he said, manacling her arm with a steel grip. "You're not going anywhere."

"Take your hands off the lady."

Aileen's stomach took an extra tumble. She looked beyond Knute to see Rhys push Abe out of the doorway.

"Or you'll what, Lindgren?" Knute asked.

Knute flipped the rifle to point it at Rhys, but Rhys was faster. He grabbed the barrel and ripped the weapon from Knute's hands.

"What the hell!" Knute muttered. "Don't you care that your own father was torn apart by some damn wolf?"

Rhys threw a punch that knocked the other man on his butt. "Let's get out of here," he growled, taking Aileen's hand and pulling her to the door.

Rhys's glare was enough motivation for Abe to get out of their way. As they passed the bar, he threw the rifle to Dave. And while the bar went silent, all eyes on them, no one tried to stop them as they exited.

As she stepped down to the sidewalk, Aileen asked, "Are you all right?"

"Unhurt," Rhys said as he pulled her down the street.

"Where are we going?"

"Back to the lodge."

But since his truck was at his cabin, they went on foot. No shortcut tonight. No conversation, either. Rhys was lost somewhere in his own head. He was going so fast talking would be difficult, anyway.

It wasn't until they were on the gravel road leading to the lodge that he finally slowed and said, "I'm going to ask Valerie to borrow one of her vehicles so I can bring you to your brother's place where you'll be safe."

"I'm not going to leave you."

"I'm not going to give you a choice."

"You're not the boss of me." As usual, Aileen got irritated when he went all alpha on her. "As a matter of fact, I'm not sure what you are to me."

"I understand."

Rhys sounded stricken, as if she'd hurt him, and quick guilt made Aileen back up. "No, Rhys, I don't think you do."

He didn't seem to realize she felt as if they were parts of the same whole. He didn't seem to feel it himself. So where did that leave her?

"You don't know what you're up against," he said. "Tonight is the full moon."

Which was already climbing high in the night sky and casting an eerie silver-blue glow over the snow. Aileen shivered. She hadn't forgotten Madam Sofia's claim that a werewolf could be made on the night of a full moon—if the victim didn't die first, of course.

Suddenly feeling cold inside, she asked, "What are you planning?"

"You don't need to know."

"I'm part of this." *Part of you.*

"You shouldn't be."

Hurt that he was trying to shut her out, Aileen agreed. "No, maybe I shouldn't." She stopped in front of the lodge. "I guess you should go do whatever it is you don't want to tell me about."

"I'm just going to be on the lookout, that's all." Rhys hesitated a second and added, "The whole pack will be. If the creature is out tonight, we'll find him."

A statement that put cold fear in her heart. What in the world did he think he and his poor wolves could do against a savage killer?

"Stay with me instead," she pleaded.

"I can't, Aileen." He touched her face, making her want to melt against him.

"You could have been killed today."

"Because I was careless. I won't be so careless again." He brushed his lips across hers. "I thank you for what you did today."

"You knew, then?"

"I knew."

The next kiss was deep, wringing from her

feelings she knew he was experiencing, as well. Her pulse thrummed intense and steady and his body echoed hers. They were one. How could he try to shut her out? Did he really think he could?

When he pulled back, Rhys's eyes glittered with emotion. "When this is over…"

He backed away from her, turned and jogged into the night.

When it was over, he could be dead!

Her heart thundered with her fear for him. If he faced the werewolf, would he survive? Wanting in the worst way to help him somehow, she knew of only one person who might be able to tell her how.

She had to see Madam Sofia.

No matter how many times she'd dealt the cards, the answer had been the same. Darkness was upon them and if she did nothing, more deaths would haunt her.

Knowing that the evil was growing in strength, that this night of both solstice and full moon offered the opportunity to harness increased power, Sofia Zak stepped from her ritual bath. She donned the pale gray silk gown with silver trim, the colors calling up strength and psychic protection. Then she loosened her silver hair from its braid and brushed it straight down her back.

Picking up a basket she'd set by the back door, she left her private quarters and moved into her snow-covered garden where her altar of white cedar doubled as her potting and harvest table. She grew and dried the herbs she sold in her shop.

From the basket, Sofia drew a pale blue cloth and laid it across the altar. Her red astral candle came next, set in the middle, then five blue tapers surrounding it, and to the side, a small white candle and silver ribbon. To the other side, she set her incense holder and added dragon's blood resin, dried mandrake and Yerba Santa. Hoping this would work, she lit the incense and waited for the odor to permeate the night air around her before invoking the goddess whose help she needed.

"Oh, Isis, be with me now in my hour of need and help me weave a skein of protection so I can battle the evil that darkens this place." Then she lit the white candle. "This candle burns in my name."

Closing her eyes for a moment so that her thoughts would be focused and potent, she called up the visage that threatened Wolf Creek. When it swirled through the mists of her mind and took form—human and yet not, wolf and yet not—she was only mildly startled. She should have known.

Opening her eyes, she lit the first blue candle. "Oh, Spirit, let strength and protection fill me."

She lit the second candle. "Oh, Earth, let strength and protection fill me." The third. Fourth. Fifth. Called on each of the elements. Tied the silver ribbon from candle to candle. "Elements of power, weave your spell and protect me."

Madam Sofia stood quietly and focused on the candles and ribbon until they radiated light that surrounded her. Then she closed her eyes again and willed the silver thread to weave its way around the threatening image, surrounding it and making it powerless.

But the thread wouldn't cooperate, and she faltered a moment.

Focusing again, she tried to form an image of the evil already surrounded by silver thread.

That didn't work, either....

And was that a smile on those curled lips between glowing yellow eyes?

Suddenly unsure of what was happening—was its power stronger than her magic? Perhaps she should have gathered her coven to do this—Sofia Zak tried telling herself she was imagining things. And then a wail directly behind her sent a chill up her spine.

"Oowoo-oo-oo-woo..."

Frozen to the spot, she fought for breath. Too late. She'd waited too long to try to contain it.

Evil was here.

Chapter Fifteen

"Valerie." Aileen stood behind the counter and waited for the owner to come out of her office. She couldn't let Rhys take such a risk without trying to help him, but she didn't want to put herself at more risk than was necessary. Rhys had given her the idea about borrowing the vehicle. "Valerie, are you there?" she called impatiently.

"Mrs. Gleiter left."

Aileen turned to see a dark-haired teenage girl sitting near the Christmas tree intent on her laptop. The girl's hands were moving furiously over the keyboard, and the computer made gaming sounds.

"Did she say when she was going to be back?"

"She didn't say anything. She was in a big hurry, though."

Aileen glanced outside. Both the lodge's truck and Valerie's SUV were parked in their usual spots. Maybe Valerie had gone for a walk. Not the smartest thing considering the recent deaths, but Valerie was no timid woman. Her only weakness seemed to be her judgment in men.

Wanting to get back to town and the herb shop as fast as she could, Aileen was desperate. "Listen, if she comes back before I do, tell her I had to see Madam Sofia. She'll understand. And tell her I'm borrowing one of her vehicles to be safe," she added in hopes that would stop Valerie from reporting it stolen. "Can you do that?"

"Yeah, sure...Madam Sofia...you're borrowing her car."

But the teenager didn't even look up from her laptop, making Aileen wonder if the message would ever reach Valerie.

Once outside, she opened the SUV door and checked for keys between the sunshade and the roof. Thankfully Valerie was a creature of habit. She climbed behind the wheel and started the engine. A last look back assured her the owner was nowhere in sight. Hopefully she would get what she needed and return before Valerie even realized the SUV was missing.

Driving straight for Caravan Herbs and Potions, she prayed Madam Sofia would be able to help her. Rhys was putting himself in danger and she was the only one who knew it. No one else would help him. No one else would care.

Except for Madam Sofia. She cared. She'd tried helping from the first. Aileen sighed. To think, less than a week ago, she'd considered the old woman's warnings as nonsense.

The storefront was dark, but when Aileen got out of the vehicle, she could see light coming through the beaded curtain that led to Madam Sofia's private quarters. She knocked at the window and waited for a moment. No response. Trying again, she held her agitation at bay as she waited. Madam Sofia had to be here. Surely the old woman had the knowledge—perhaps even the means—to uncover and stop the werewolf before something happened to Rhys. She couldn't lose him now. She wouldn't!

Still no response.

Aileen repositioned herself in front of the door and tried to see all the way back through the shop and through the beaded curtain. A futile effort. She couldn't tell if Madam Sofia was home or not. The woman was elderly—maybe her hearing wasn't that good.

What now? Frustration made her smack the door with the flat of her hand...and the door creaked open a crack.

The breath caught in Aileen's throat and blood pulsed unevenly through her veins. Reaching out, she pushed and the door opened wider.

"Madam Sofia?" she called out loudly, torn about what to do when there was no answer.

What if Madam Sofia was in trouble and needed help?

A quick look down the street showed it was deserted. No one she could ask to go inside with her. She could call someone. Who? Not the authorities—she didn't trust Sheriff Caine. For all she knew, he *was* the danger. Valerie was AWOL. And Donovan was at home with his family in Iron Lake. No doubt her brother would come if she asked, but it would take him a while to get here.

What if Madam Sophia had become ill and time was of the essence?

She had to investigate…she owed it to the woman.

Her heart in her throat, Aileen took a cautious step inside the darkened shop. She stopped. Listened. Heard nothing. Sensed no other presence. That was good. So she headed for the parlor where they'd had tea.

The room was deserted. Aileen kept going, entering the well-lit but empty kitchen. The counter was scattered with bits of herbs and boxes of candles and strands of ribbon, as though Sofia had recently been working furiously in here. But then what?

Perhaps Sofia had gone out and had been forgetful about the front door. Aileen was about to leave when a pale fluttering from outside the window caught her eye. Frowning, she moved closer to see what it was.

A garment of some sort…

"Oh, no! Madam Sofia!"

Pulling the door open, Aileen rushed outside.

Backed by an altar lit with the remainders of burning candles, Madam Sofia lay on her back, her limbs sprawled, her eyes wide open and unfocused. It was as if she were the centerpiece of some sacrificial ceremony. The blood covering the front of her silver gown looked black in the moonlight.

Aileen moved closer and her stomach clutched when she saw Madam Sofia's throat ripped open.

The poor woman…

Shaking, willing herself not to throw up, Aileen backed away from the body and looked around wildly. What did she do now? The only person who might have had the knowledge or means to stop the werewolf had just become its latest victim. And the victims were now mounting fast, which meant everyone in Wolf Creek might be doomed.

Rhys needed to be told about Madam Sofia. Hopefully he would come up with a plan.

Rhys, I need you…why did you have to go alone…

Aileen found her cell, but before she could put the call through, a growl from close behind stopped her. The phone tumbled from her suddenly numb fingers to the frozen ground. Her insides gripped tight as in a vise, her heartbeat a rapid tattoo. Slowly, she turned to face what looked like a gray wolf.

Only this one was bigger and more muscular and seemingly more dangerous than any she'd ever encountered. It growled and snarled at her, and bloody froth—Madam Sofia's blood!—dripped from its jaws.

The werewolf!

Her mind racing for a way out, Aileen avoided the creature's glowing yellow eyes so as not to challenge it. That might give her a few extra seconds to find a weapon. Her stomach twisted and her chest hurt simply from trying to breathe. She had no idea of the creature's awareness—whether it thought like animal or man—no idea of how to fight it.

Wait—her pouch!

Reaching into her pocket, she found nothing. Empty. Telling herself not to panic, she tried the other pocket. Tape recorder. Still no pouch. It must have fallen out and she hadn't noticed.

Which meant no wolfsbane. Which meant no protection against the supernatural creature that now stalked her.

Rhys, where are you? It's here...it's here...

If only he could hear her, could feel the connection that made them as one. She tried to latch on to him psychically, but she couldn't sense anything. No vibes. No blood pulsing except her own in fear.

With frozen limbs, she backed up slowly, avoiding stepping on Madam Sofia's body, and drew closer to the altar and the candles that still burned there.

Fire...drawing on the legends, she remembered fire could stop a werewolf...

It moved with her, its jaws widening as if in a grin. As if it knew what she was planning and was amused at her attempt to escape.

Not daring to give the werewolf her back, Aileen carefully reached behind her, found the edge of the altar and slid her hand to one of the candles and wrapped her fingers around its base. A sudden fierce growl startled her. Her hand jerked and knocked over the candle. The creature bunched its muscles even as the hot wax poured over her flesh, pain stopping her from fleeing.

"A-a-aah!" she yelled.

The werewolf launched itself into the air and she fell backward, the descent broken momentarily when her head snapped against a sharp edge.

Then downward she slid, trying to focus, trying

to fight the darkness that rapidly swept over her as she felt the werewolf's rancid breath on her face.

NO SIGN OF THE CREATURE. He and the pack had been patrolling their territory with no results. Not so much as a single scent. A single intuition as to where it could be.

But some other sense alerted him to danger. Not here in the woods. Not to the pack.

Aileen...

The connection was faint, but it pulsed with fear greater than he'd ever experienced. She was in trouble. He knew it. He stopped and concentrated, but got nothing more, as if her consciousness had abruptly ceased.

Without thinking, he raced through the woods toward Gray Wolf Lodge where he had left her. She had to be all right...had to be...couldn't lose her...

Aileen, I'm coming...

He ran as fast as he could go, his long legs eating the distance, his focus on one thing only. And only when he came in sight of the lodge some time later did he slow near a stand of trees behind the equipment shed to get his breath.

Aileen. The lodge. She had to be there.

He started off again, slower this time, this time

with a plan. Approaching the back of the building, he targeted her deck.

Then with a burst of speed and strength, he ran several yards and leaped up...up...up...and caught onto the railing. He scrabbled over onto the deck and pressed his nose to the glass.

She wasn't inside. He didn't sense her.

Closing his eyes, he concentrated, envisioned hands and feet, arms and legs. His human body. His blood raced until heat enveloped him. He swallowed the cry of pain that always infused him when he transformed. Feeling as if every nerve were on fire, every bone shattered, he stretched and shifted and settled into human form.

Disoriented as always, he stumbled against the rail and for a moment just stood there, clinging to the support. Then he took a deep breath and tried the door. The fact that it was locked didn't stop him. He practically tore the door from its hinges.

Stepping inside, he attuned his senses to the room, which was faint with her scent. She hadn't been here for hours, certainly not since he'd dropped her off.

How in the hell was he going to find her?

Valerie.

About to leave the room to find the owner, his boot nicked some object that skittered across the floor. He looked down.

Aileen's protection pouch.

His heart thumped harder. No protection.

No...

Picking up the pouch, he shoved it in his pocket and went in search of the lodge owner. He took the stairs down two at a time. A few guests were gathered in the common room. No Valerie. He went behind the counter and checked her office. Not there, either.

Fighting panic, he asked, "Does anyone know where to find Valerie Gleiter?"

"Mrs. Gleiter left a long time ago."

His gaze went straight to the girl by the Christmas tree. She was focused on her laptop.

"Do you know where she went?"

"Like I told the other woman, no."

Rhys approached her, tried to keep his voice even so he wouldn't scare her into silence. "What other woman?"

"I dunno."

"Did she have blond hair?"

Intent on her game, the girl shrugged. "Maybe."

"Do you know where she went?"

Maddeningly, the teenager still didn't look up from her computer. "Madam someone. And, oh yeah, she said to say she borrowed a car."

Sensing he wasn't going to get any more

details, Rhys left. He had to get to Madam Sofia's fast and his own truck was back at the cabin. He jogged to the lodge's truck. People around here were trusting enough to leave the keys in their vehicles. Finding the key ring between the sunshade and roof, grateful for his luck, he took off immediately.

His urgency didn't abate, not even when he arrived in front of Caravan Herbs and Potions. The shop door was open and a scent that squeezed his gut was on the wind.

The scent of blood...

In less than a minute he was through the shop, through Sofia's private quarters and in the garden. His heart nearly stopped when he saw the body, but upon realizing it wasn't Aileen, his pulse picked up speed.

He stood over Madam Sofia and said a silent prayer for the soul of the kind old woman—another thing Father had taught him.

"I will stop the one who did this to you, Madam Sofia," he promised. "And Father. And the other victims." He could only hope that would happen before it was too late for Aileen.

He took just enough time to get impressions from the garden. Aileen had been here not long ago—her scent lingered around the altar. As did that of the werewolf...

Rhys stopped and tuned into his sense of smell. He'd never picked up the werewolf's scent when it was this fresh before.

Why was it so familiar? he wondered.

Why did it make him think of Valerie Gleiter?

AILEEN GROANED AS SHE fought her way to consciousness through a haze of hurt. The back of her head throbbed. As did her burned hand. And her muscles were stiff and uncooperative. She felt as if she could hardly move, like half her body was asleep.

Groaning, she attempted to move her right arm.

"So you're awake."

Her eyes flicked open. She was in a moving vehicle on a dark road. Groaning again, she muttered, "What happened?"

"You were playing hero and got hurt."

The deep voice that rumbled at her was unfamiliar. She squinted at him. He was big—both tall and muscular. His hair and beard looked to be peppered with gray. She'd never met him and yet she thought she'd seen him before somewhere. Had he been in one of her dreams?

She asked, "You saved me from the werewolf?"

His laugher jerked her further awake. "Is that what you think?"

She didn't know what to think. The last she remembered… "Okay, wolf, then," she said. "Did you kill it?"

"I *am* it, honey." He glanced her way and grinned at her, and she swore his canines glinted in the dark.

Her breath caught in her throat. He wasn't kidding. He was the creature in human form. He'd torn out Madam Sofia's throat. And Jens's. He'd nearly ripped Fisk apart. And she was trapped with him.

She had to get out of the truck, had to get away. But when she tried to edge her hand toward the door to find the handle, she realized why she hadn't been able to move her arm before. It wasn't because it had gone to sleep. Rather, both hands were tied together behind her back.

"W-what do you want with me?" Why hadn't he killed her like he had Madam Sofia?

"I'm looking for a woman with spirit, one who isn't afraid of the supernatural."

For what purpose?

Not wanting to go there, she swallowed hard. "Who said I'm not afraid?"

He laughed again. "If you were, you wouldn't be hanging out with the likes of Rhys Lindgren, would you?"

"What do you know about Rhys?"

He didn't answer her question, just laughed

again. "I need a new female and since you're so attracted to wolves, you'll be perfect. But first I need to show you what happens to unfaithful mates so you don't get out of line."

Her stomach knotted. "Unfaithful?"

"That bitch Valerie has been spreading it around."

"Valerie?" Aileen started. It couldn't be… She took a better look at him. Remembered the lodge brochure she'd seen the day she arrived. No wonder he looked familiar. "You're Magnus Gleiter? But you're—"

"Dead?" he supplied. "Not everyone knows how to do a job right."

Aileen took a shaky breath and tried to wake herself up. Surely this one of her dreams. A nightmare. But, no, she was fully awake.

Magnus stopped the vehicle in front of a cabin. As he dragged her out, she realized he'd brought her in Valerie's SUV. How appropriate.

He marched her toward the door and rather than knocking, kicked it open.

Pouring water into a cup, Valerie dropped the kettle and flipped around. "Magnus!"

He shoved Aileen into a wooden chair. "Surprise, honey, I'm home!"

"I—I knew it…so you did kill Fisk?"

"More than Fisk," he said.

"Too bad you didn't die."

Magnus was concentrating on his wife and had his back to Aileen, which gave her some wiggle room. If only she could free her hands, she could run out and drive the SUV for help. She wasn't foolish enough to think she could overpower Magnus, not even with Valerie's help.

"You would have had to blow my brains out if you really wanted me dead," Magnus told his wife. "Or you should have cut off my head so I couldn't rise again."

"That was months ago," Valerie was saying. "Nearly a year. Why come back now?"

Having found a piece of metal sticking out from the back of the chair, Aileen caught the rope on it and pulled. Scraping her burned skin, she caught her breath and waited for the pain to recede.

"You think coming back was easy?" Magnus asked. "It took me days to emerge from the ground, weeks to heal and get to someplace safe, months to rebuild my strength. But now I'm myself again, and I've had a lot of time to think of creative ways to make you suffer before you die."

They were arguing to the point of forgetting she was there, Aileen realized as she scrunched up her good hand and tried working it through the loop she'd loosened a bit.

"Bastard! You deserve to be dead for the things you did to me!" Valerie said, her voice shaking. "I would never have come near you if I'd known what you were. I'm just thankful you never got me pregnant."

Magnus laughed. "You won't have children with anyone else, either. Not ever."

Valerie lunged to the side and tried to get past him, but Magnus grabbed her and hit her with all his strength so she flew across the room and into a cabinet that shuddered against the wall. Magnus stalked her and Valerie picked up a small table and held it between them.

"You think that twig is going to stop me?" he boomed just as the cabin door banged open on its hinges once more.

Aileen's heart hammered against her ribs.

Rhys stood on the other side.

Chapter Sixteen

Now Rhys knew why the killer's scent had reminded him of Valerie. He associated the man with his reluctant wife. One quick glance assured him that Aileen sat unharmed, her hands secured behind her. Thankfully, he hadn't lost another person he loved. Yet.

"Rhys!" she cried. "Be careful, he's the killer!"

The creature flipped around, then cocked his head like a wolf and grinned. "Lindgren, just in time to make things interesting."

"Magnus Gleiter, back from the dead."

Envisioning Father with his throat ripped out—and Patterson, Oeland and Madam Sofia—Rhys knew he had to do whatever it took to stop the killer from striking again.

The moon was full tonight...

"What are you going to do about it, Lindgren?"

"Let me think."

Without taking his eyes off Gleiter, Rhys

slipped Aileen's protection pouch from his jacket pocket into hers. Then, pulling the leather thong from his neck, he removed the even stronger protection Madam Sofia had created for him to keep his darker side in check. The full moon immediately clouded his thoughts, and his image of Gleiter was enveloped in a haze of red. His pulse beat in strong strokes and all his senses heightened. The urge to transform grew stronger.

"It's time to put you back in the ground where you belong, Gleiter."

With a roar, Magnus tore away from Valerie and lunged for Rhys. Lighter and quicker, Rhys avoided the collision. He kicked out, got Magnus in the back of the knee so his leg gave and he stumbled.

Magnus fell to the floor, turned and hooked a foot behind Rhys's ankle. He, too, went down but rolled out of Magnus's way. Magnus was fast for a big man, and he leaped on Rhys before he could get up.

"Let's make this interesting," he growled, his form stretching and changing.

"Let's not!"

Rhys punched Gleiter in the gut, slowing his transformation. Stuck in a nightmare, halfway between human and wolf, Gleiter snapped his distended jaws around Rhys's neck. Rhys felt the teeth sink into him and howled as he got his hands around the werewolf's neck and squeezed and squeezed until the jaws loosened.

Something crashed down on the creature, making him fall back. Through his haze of fury, Rhys saw Aileen standing over them, what was left of the chair in her hands.

Rhys got to his feet and shoved her out of danger's way even as the creature shimmered and completed the transformation. Rhys didn't want to transform, didn't want to lose the last of his conscious will.

"Rhys!" Valerie yelled. "Catch!"

The moment he looked up to see her in front of the open weapons cabinet, she tossed a knife to him. His reflexes sharp, he caught it by the handle, and as the werewolf sprang, Rhys flipped it around and drove the blade in through the creature's ribs in the area of its heart.

The werewolf's howl pierced Rhys's ears and charged his inner nature. His blood pounded and his nerves were on fire. He wanted to rip his opponent open until he bled to death. It took all his conscious will not to turn...

He stood panting...focused on his human form...as the werewolf fell to the ground and bucked...

His limbs stretched, starting to change shape...

"No!" he growled, looking down at his hands that were curling...changing... "No!"

And then he felt it. A wave of something inexplicably calm washed over him. He grasped onto it, became one with it. The urge to transform receded.

Startled, he looked to Aileen, her blue eyes bright with unshed tears. Standing several yards away, she had focused her entire being on him. Before he could analyze what had just happened, a loud blast reverberated through the cabin, sending shards of pain through his ears into his brain.

Valerie stood over the werewolf, shotgun in hand. She'd blown the creature's brains to bits.

"He won't rise again this time," Valerie vowed, dropping the weapon and throwing herself into a stunned Rhys's arms. "Thank you, thank you! You saved my life."

And before he knew what was happening, she was kissing him. Blood rushing through his veins in a way that put him off, he pushed her away. "Valerie—"

"You and I belong together, Rhys. I can deal with you and your two forms. You're a good man, not a monster like Magnus was, and I put up with him for years."

So Gleiter had told her what he'd done, Rhys realized. "I'm not available," he said, seeking out an uncertain-looking Aileen, who had backed away as she watched them.

"Magnus already ruined my life. Do you want to ruin hers, as well?" Before he could tell her he would never do that, Valerie said, "Not only will you outlive her, but you won't be able to give her children, and she told me she wants kids. Would you take that away from her?"

Aileen didn't say anything. She seemed oddly distant....

Children...he'd never thought that far. He only knew he loved Aileen, that he would be lost without her. But maybe that wasn't enough for her. More important, maybe he was too much. Tonight had proved that.

Keeping his emotions at bay, Rhys picked up his protection pouch and hung it over his neck. Then he checked what looked like the remains of an ordinary wolf. "Let's hope his carcass satisfies the authorities."

"What about the autopsies?" Aileen asked. She, too, was focusing on what was left of Gleiter. "You know they'll do one and compare the saliva to what they found on the wounds of the dead men. They'll match...but what kind of conclusions are they going to draw from his saliva? It won't be the same as that of a natural wolf."

"Certainly not the truth. Let's hope they think they've found some unusual virus that attacked the wolf's brain and that they leave it at that." Whatever strange disease made Gleiter into a lycanthrope wouldn't be recognized as such, not when only a handful of people believed a werewolf actually existed. "Then maybe they'll leave the wolves alone."

"More likely the DNR will trap a bunch and test them," Aileen said.

"That doesn't mean the wolves will die, though."

"I'll talk to Donovan right away, see what kind of influence he can exert."

Only one thing was certain, Rhys thought. The werewolf who had made him was dead at last.

THEY HAD THEIR STORY STRAIGHT by the time Sheriff Caine, an EMT and one of the DNR men arrived.

Having already called Donovan and told him what really happened, having elicited from her brother a promise that he would cover for them if necessary and would make sure nothing lethal was done to the wolves, having made an anonymous call to the sheriff's office about Sofia Zak being dead, Aileen was still plagued by a continuing sense of dread.

Valerie was leaving the cabin when the wolf appeared, they told the sheriff.

Rhys and Aileen were taking a short walk when they heard her scream. They came running and saw Valerie holding the wolf off with a small table.

And then the rest of their story was pretty factual in the order of what happened to whom. Rhys's bite wound treated by the paramedic was a visual detail that pretty much sealed their account.

"A doctor should look at this." The paramedic finished bandaging Rhys's neck. "I can take you to the E.R."

"I think I'll wait until morning," Rhys said. "I'm too tired to stay up all night waiting for some overworked doctor to have a look. I can see my own doctor tomorrow."

Though Aileen knew he wouldn't unless he were forced. He'd told her that, as severe as it was, the wound would heal fast. Indeed, by the time the paramedic had arrived, he had seemed to be on the mend.

At Rhys's insistence, the paramedic took care of her burned hand and told her it would be fine in a couple of days.

And through this, Sheriff Caine was watching. "So one of your wolves was at fault, after all."

"Not one of my wolves," Rhys countered. "A disperser. His own pack kicked him out."

Which, in a way, was true.

"I didn't see your truck out there," Caine said. "I can give you a ride back to your cabin."

"Not necessary. I'm going to see Aileen to the lodge."

In the end, after everyone else left, Valerie drove them. "No way am I going to stay in that cabin alone tonight," she said with a shudder. "Maybe never again."

And when they got inside, the owner went right to her office and Aileen wondered what Rhys was waiting for. Why didn't he take her in his arms and kiss her and tell her he loved her and everything would be all right? Wasn't that part of her grandmother's legacy? A happy ending?

RHYS FOLLOWED AILEEN TO her room but stopped in the doorway, a deep gloom settling over him. He knew what he had to do. For her.

"What is it?" she asked.

"I should go."

"No. Please don't leave. Come in." Her expression was at once hopeful and anxious. "You belong with me."

"I never should have gotten involved with you in the first place, not when I don't even understand where I belong in this world. I can't give you what you need, Aileen."

She said, "I need *you*," and he did step inside. He had to make her understand that he was no good for her.

When she reached around him to close the door, her scent filled him with desire. He wanted to lift her in his arms and throw her on the bed and take her all night. Resisting was the hardest thing he'd ever done. Harder than not turning when the bloodlust had been upon him earlier.

"We have no future together. You have to see that. I can't give you a normal life, Aileen. Certainly no kids. I'm sure Valerie was right about that."

"You're enough for me now." She moved into him, touched his face. "I'm not making any demands. And the future will take care of itself."

He cupped his hand over hers and twined their fingers together. "You'd be standing guard over me like Father did every time there's a full moon. I can't curse you like that."

"That's not your decision to make alone. And you didn't turn tonight, not even when you took off the protection. You're stronger, more in control, than you think."

"Don't you understand?" How could she not see it? The impossibility. The thing Father had most feared for him was that he would lose his heart to this woman that he couldn't have. "I'm not like other men."

"I don't care how you define yourself. You're nothing like Magnus Gleiter. I love you. Who you are…what you are…you're what I want."

His resistance gave way. He pulled her to him and took possession of her mouth. There was no other woman for him. She was his alpha. She made his blood pound and sing at the same time. And at the same time heat seared him, his nerves began twitching and muscles stretching. The protection pouch seemed useless against Aileen. Wanting her so badly was making him lose control….

Even as he fought transformation, Rhys pushed her away.

"Leave, Aileen." He rushed to the deck door that hung crookedly on its hinges from where he'd ripped it open earlier. "Take the first bus out in the morning and don't look back."

As he moved, his limbs stretched, changed shape. Heat and unbearable pain drove him into the cold. He looked back once to see heartbreak sketched on Aileen's face before he let himself go and leaped over the railing.

By the time he hit ground, he was running on all fours.

His destiny. Not hers.

NOT BOTHERING TO UNDRESS, Aileen threw herself on the bed. She tried to sleep…needed to dream…

wanted some clue as to what she was supposed to do next…as to how she was supposed to convince Rhys that he was wrong.

Sleep and dreams and solutions eluded her, and in the middle of the night she found herself replaying everything she knew about the killings in her mind.

Rhys thought Magnus turned him, but Magnus hadn't used that fact against him. She could swear Magnus was bigger and had different coloring than the wolf who'd attacked her and the black wolf in her dreams. Time could have changed him, and he could have aged, of course, turned more silvery.

He may have been the killer, but what if he hadn't been responsible for turning Rhys? Was there still a threat in their midst?

Aileen didn't trust Sheriff Caine…and what about Valerie herself? All three had been in Canada together. Madam Sofia had said the werewolf came from the north and worked its way here from Canada with the wolves. Had Magnus been the only one? Thoughts that wouldn't let her alone.

Wandering down to the common room, she wasn't surprised to find Valerie sitting in the dark except for the Christmas tree lights and the fire. And a couple of lit table candles that reminded her of the sacrificial candles on Madam Sofia's altar. Aileen shuddered. A brandy snifter in hand, Valerie sat staring into the fireplace as if she were looking for answers.

"Still up?"

"Couldn't sleep," Valerie said. "Seems to be catching. Have a drink. The tray's on the counter. I should've just brought the bottle here. There won't be anything left by morning, anyway."

"You're almost empty now," Aileen said, taking the snifter from her. "Let me get you a refill."

"Thanks."

Aileen set a fresh glass next to Valerie's. Glancing back to make sure the other woman wasn't watching her, she prepared the drinks. Valerie had already had a lot of brandy. Aileen hoped she was relaxed enough to talk.

"Here you go." After handing Valerie her refill, Aileen sat in the chair next to the Christmas tree. Something normal in a suddenly abnormal world. "Do you have any idea what you're going to do now?"

Emptying half her snifter, Valerie echoed, "Do? What's there to do? I'm still in the same prison. We're the only ones who know Magnus is dead. I'm stuck here unless I find some way out."

Valerie downed the other half and settled back into the couch, closing her eyes. Her breathing slowed and the tension seemed to drain from her body. Aileen was almost convinced the other woman was asleep when Valerie began to giggle.

"Something's funny?"

"My life," Valerie said. "All I've ever wanted was to have control over it, and that's the one thing I've never had." Her laugh remained giddy. Unnatural. "I thought Magnus was my ticket to a different life from the hell that I escaped. He was. Just not the one I'd envisioned." Her words slurred a bit. "A different kind of hell."

"You said before that he changed your life and you could never go back…"

At Aileen's prompt, Valerie focused for a moment. Their gazes locked and Aileen wondered if she'd pushed too far. Had she put herself in danger?

Then Valerie said, "Magnus didn't ask me if I wanted it, you know. He just did it."

"Did what?"

"Turned me," she admitted. "I was so naive, I didn't know what he was until then."

Aileen held her breath. The drink was working far better than she'd imagined. Or maybe it was Magnus's death that was making Valerie open up.

"At first I couldn't control the rage and hunger and so went out to kill anything I could."

"Anything?"

Again, the measuring look. "Did Rhys tell you

how we met? Or does he even know. Oh, wait."
Valerie shook a finger at Aileen. "You were
the-e-re," she sing-songed. That *was* you, wasn't
it?"

"Yes."

"Took me a while to figure it out. I knew you
smelled familiar the day you got here, but that
perfume confused me." Valerie sobered when she
said, "I apologize if I hurt you. I was out of
control." Her eyes welled with tears. "I never
wanted to hurt anyone. The next day when I
realized what I'd become, I tried to kill myself.
Not so easy when you have supernatural healing
powers. Then I vowed I wouldn't kill any human,
ever. I tried to control the hunger. I really did. I
locked myself up at every full moon. If he could
find me, Magnus would let me out and then laugh
at me the next day. I couldn't remember anything,
but he made me look at what I did to my kill.
Made me face what I'd really become."

How truly sadistic Magnus Gleiter had been.
Aileen felt a wave of sorrow wash over her. What
was going to happen to Valerie now? Could
Aileen really keep this information to herself?
On the other hand, she didn't have details, didn't
have proof that Valerie had actually killed anyone.
And obviously poor Valerie hadn't been respon-
sible for her actions.

"You have no idea of the things Magnus did to

me," Valerie went on. "I hated him for condemning me to this godforsaken life, cursing me to be swayed by my cycles, always fighting the urge to kill when the moon was full, desperate to breed without the hope of a term pregnancy." She giggled again. "You want to talk biological clock, you have no clue of how bad it can be if you're like me…and the joke was on me, too, because Magnus was sterile."

Wanting to hear it all before Valerie sobered up, Aileen asked, "What happened last year before Magnus disappeared?"

"We'd had a huge fight. He finally figured out that I'd gone to Sofia Zak for help so that I wouldn't go out of control again."

"So that's why he killed Madam Sofia."

"He never forgot, never forgave." Valerie shook her head and her voice grew quieter, more mournful when she said, "Magnus took away the protection she made for me and tried to convince me to kill with him for sport. I couldn't take it anymore. I told him I was leaving him. He beat me and said he would never let me go. That I was condemned to this life forever, and that it would be a very, very long life. Magnus was in his seventies, you know. I'm nearly forty myself."

Having thought the woman was younger than she, Aileen was shocked into silence for a moment. When she regained her voice, she asked, "So you tried to kill him to get away?"

"I thought I had." Valerie got very quiet now and her eyes glistened with remembering. "I did it when he was sleeping. And then I buried him in the woods. Since then, I've turned to kinder men, men who I thought could father my children. They impregnated me, but each time I miscarried. That's why I want Rhys. He can give me what I need. My children would outlive me."

Rhys...

A lump in her throat, Aileen thought of him, of the fact that he probably could give Valerie the children she so desperately needed...but couldn't do the same for her. Aileen could live with that—she'd despaired of ever finding a soul mate until she'd met him—but apparently he couldn't.

"You never thought about turning one of your lovers?"

"And condemn them to what I've gone through in the process? Death was kinder, don't you think?"

Valerie sounded as though she regretted those deaths, but Aileen felt a mounting sense of horror. "Wait a minute. I thought Magnus killed them."

"He killed poor Fisk. And Madam Sofia."

"But not Tom Patterson or the other two men? Or Jens?"

"They all knew too much about me. When I

miscarried, my lovers were a danger to my survival. And Jens found them…what was left of my babies." Tears spilled from Valerie's eyes and washed down her cheeks. "The old bastard dug them up and was going to hand them over to the authorities and tell them to match the DNA with the dead men. I couldn't let him do it. I wasn't going to be hunted and killed or caged." Valerie slashed at her tears. "Now I know I need a mate who is both human and wolf, like me. Rhys is kind and has ethics and morals. The perfect father…"

"You'll never have Rhys, because he's mine." Aileen pictured him in her mind and tried to send him the message she conveyed to Valerie. Tried to make him feel the connection that had started all those years ago. He couldn't turn his back on it. Couldn't turn his back on *her.* "Alphas mate for life."

Valerie snorted. "You know I really like you, Aileen, but you're not like me and Rhys. As a matter of fact, you're not an alpha anything."

"Simply because I'm a less volatile person doesn't mean I'm not strong, that I don't have power of my own." Aileen challenged her. "You can't have Rhys."

Rhys was hers. Nothing would change her mind. She pictured them together…in each other's arms…making love. Mentally she called to him, begged him to see the honest truth about how she felt. She didn't want to be without him.

Valerie's expression turned dark and suddenly she sounded sober. "You know, it's too bad you have this attitude. I thought you understood me, what I've been through…."

And then the other woman's features hardened and Aileen saw that she was trying to concentrate, trying to turn. A frisson of fear skittered through Aileen, and she concentrated on Rhys more fiercely. She willed him to come back.

Valerie's limbs stretched and then went back to normal. She tried again, but no matter how hard she tried, she couldn't seem to manage the transformation.

"I don't understand…it's a full moon…"

"Give up, Valerie. I laced your drink with wolfsbane."

Their gazes locked.

"You *poisoned* me?"

"Not poisoned. It was a tincture of wolfsbane, not full strength. It'll just keep you human for the time being."

Valerie's fury was palpable. Her face went red and her eyes glistened. Grabbing Aileen's full snifter, she tossed the contents at her, dousing Aileen with the brandy.

Aileen flew up out of her seat. "Valerie, please calm down! I'm not trying to hurt you."

But Valerie didn't listen as she reached out and knocked the lit candle in Aileen's direction.

Chapter Seventeen

Aileen ducked and the candle flew straight into the Christmas tree behind her. Flames flickered and shot up, and within seconds the dry pine combusted. If she hadn't been quick-witted, that would have been her.

"Oh, no!" Valerie flew out of her seat and began hitting the flaming tree with an afghan. Rather than put out the blaze, the material caught on fire, so she threw the afghan to the side where it burned unhindered.

"Where's a fire extinguisher?" Aileen asked.

"Behind the desk."

Valerie picked up a pillow to bat at the flames as Aileen ran and got the extinguisher. By the time she figured out how it worked, the fire had spread. She did her best to put it out—they both did—but with all the old wood in the lodge, the fire hopped, skipped and jumped in every direction and fed itself until it seemed there was no way out for them.

"Why isn't the sprinkler system working?" Valerie cried. "I'm going to lose everything!"

Aileen looked around. "You're right. We're going to lose our lives. We're trapped!" They couldn't get near the front door or any other exit. The fire surrounded them. Maybe they had one chance. "If we can break the window right there," she said, pointing to a clear path, "we can get out!"

Valerie picked up a bulky wood-and-leather chair as easily as if it were her purse. She seemed ready to fling it through the window when she froze and dropped it.

"This is all your fault!" Valerie snarled. "It's all going to be gone. Everything I tried to hold on to. Gone…all gone!"

Aileen grabbed Valerie's arm and shook her. "Stop this, Valerie, or neither of us will get out alive."

"Alive? What do you think they would do to me once you tell them what I am? What I've done? How long do you think they'd let me live?"

Valerie had a point, of course. Though she was Magnus's victim, she wouldn't be allowed to get away with the murders. Then again, would anyone believe the truth?

Suddenly, fire alarms in the dining area went off and the sprinkler system went on in the common room and the area was instantly filled with smoke. Screams and shouts from around the lodge assured Aileen the guests had awakened. Footsteps tromped overhead.

Valerie looked panicked. A trapped animal. She backed away from Aileen, saying. "I can't do it! I can't be hunted and caged. If I have to live in hell, then I'll get there myself. Save yourself, Aileen!" Valerie said, after which she whipped straight into the fire. Wreathed in smoke and flames, she let out an ear-piercing scream.

"Valerie!" Fumes seared Aileen's lungs and she began to choke as a screaming Valerie burned.

She couldn't reach the other woman, couldn't save her. There was nothing she could do but watch in revulsion. And try to save herself. She tried lifting one of the smaller tables to throw at the windows, but she could barely lift the thing. Refusing to share the other woman's fate, Aileen kept looking for a way out.

Then she felt it. The shift inside her. The connection live.

Rhys…

A splintering crash of glass pulled her attention to the black wolf that broke through the window and through the flames. It shimmered and stretched and when it touched down it was a man again.

"Rhys! You came!"

He lifted her into his arms as easily as if she were a feather and shot back through a break in the fire and out through the shattered window. Guests were already milling outside and more were coming from various exits, many retreating to the safety of their vehicles.

A horrified Aileen clung to Rhys and was grateful he held her tight as Gray Wolf Lodge burned.

WHILE THE AUTHORITIES seemed to accept Aileen's story that the fire was an accident, that didn't preclude an official investigation, including the reason the sensors in the common room didn't signal the sprinkler system until it was too late. State arson investigators were already on the scene in addition to several EMT teams. Everyone who'd been in the building needed to be checked. Aileen was still coughing up soot, and while she let one of the paramedics check her out, she refused to be taken anywhere away from Rhys.

Especially not when Sheriff Caine was present and looking at them both with suspicion. "Really odd that Sofia Zak, that wolf and Valerie Gleiter all died in the same night."

He aimed his comment at her rather than at Rhys. Which made sense, she told herself, because she'd been in the burning building.

"Valerie was very upset after what happened earlier. She started drinking right away. She was so drunk she didn't know what she was doing when she knocked into the table and set the brandy on fire."

She only hoped the investigators wouldn't be able to tell the fire had started with the Christmas tree. How they could when that section of the lodge was devastated, she wasn't sure, but it worried her some.

"Unusual, too, that you were at two of the three scenes. It was only two, wasn't it?" he asked. "Forensics isn't going to find anything indicating you went to see Sofia Zak tonight. The anonymous tip we got on her came from a woman."

Her heart thudded. The way he was looking at her…as if he knew the truth. If he were another werewolf and had gone over there himself, he would have been able to pick up her scent.

"Aileen and I were together like I told you earlier," Rhys said, locking gazes with the sheriff. "I'll vouch for her."

Once again, Aileen had that sense of two alphas squaring off and it made her very, very nervous. She swore the scent of testosterone filled the air. "Can we leave now, Sheriff? We've had a really long, exhausting night."

"You can go. But don't leave town."

"I'm not planning on it," Aileen assured him.

They took Valerie's SUV back to Rhys's cabin where he made them scrambled eggs and toast.

"You said something before about Caine being in with the Gleiters," Rhys said as they finished eating. "You think he's one of them?"

While waiting for the authorities, Aileen had told Rhys the truth about Valerie and what had driven her to kill those men—including his father. Apparently, he still wasn't satisfied.

"I would say it's likely that Caine is a werewolf, except Valerie didn't choose him to father a child with her. And obviously there had been something between them in Canada."

"Maybe he was just too much like her husband for her."

That could be. Valerie had wanted Rhys because he was the opposite of Magnus. "I don't know. And is he a killer? I don't know that, either. The deaths we do know about are all accounted for between Magnus and Valerie."

"I'll be keeping an eye on Caine from now on."

"Be careful, Rhys." Aileen set down her fork. "He's no one to fool with. If he has something to hide like Valerie…"

She wasn't over the fact that in the heat of anger a woman who'd admitted to liking her— and for whom Aileen had felt something in return—had tried to set her on fire. Sheriff Caine would be a far more dangerous adversary.

Putting the dishes in the sink, Rhys said, "You should try to sleep a while before I drive you to your brother's place."

Aileen rose and walked to the windows to stare out at the forest and wondered how it had ever scared her when there were far more dangerous things afoot. "I'm not leaving."

"You have no place to stay." He stood close behind her, his breath ruffling her hair. "The lodge just burned, remember."

"I want to stay with you," she said, turning to face him, to look deep into his amber eyes. "I never want to leave."

"That doesn't make sense. After all the things that have happened in the last few days, you should run as far from me as fast as you can."

"I don't want to run. Can't you see we're meant for each other, Rhys? When I was in trouble, I mentally called and you came for me. You can't deny that connection."

"Coincidence."

"You know it's not. Rhys, I can't stand to think of you as lonely and desperate as Valerie was. You have too many decades to spend alone. And I want to be with you, to share what time I can with you. Let me keep you company."

"I'm not like you."

"You are in every way that's important to me."

"And I don't remember anything before this," he said, indicating the cabin.

"It doesn't matter how you started your life, only how you live it," Aileen insisted, drawing closer to him, placing her hands on his chest near his heart. She could feel the rhythm change under her palms, and soon her pulse was in sync with his. "I love you. I've always loved you with some part of my mind since the night you saved my life."

Memories flooded her. Her crying into the black wolf's wounds. His licking her scraped hand. And as if Rhys remembered, too—or perhaps read her thoughts—his eyes widened and his determined expression softened.

"I love you, too," he finally said, longing in his voice.

Aileen smiled. "You are Gran's gift to me, her legacy. I will never love another."

His kiss was everything she'd hoped for. He might still resist the notion that he deserved to be happy, but now that she was certain of his love, she would see that it was so.

He picked her up and carried her to his sleigh bed where they tumbled together in a delicious tangle of limbs. Aileen laughed and Rhys actually smiled before undressing her.

He nuzzled her neck and groaned. "I never want to be without you."

Aileen wondered if he was thinking of the long life he would have. "You don't ever have to be without me," she murmured. "All you have to do is bite me."

Epilogue

It was a McKenna Christmas. Rather, a McKenna Christmas Eve, the first of several days her family would spend together.

So many people, so much noise, so much love in one place.

Aileen couldn't be happier as she introduced Rhys to Laurel and Willow and to her brother Skelly and his wife, Roz. Their triplets Bridget, Brendan and Briana were first-graders now, and it did her heart good to see joy on their faces and laughter on their lips as they whipped around Donovan's big house and peeked under the tree to inspect the growing mountain of presents.

She spotted her father picking up Willow, who immediately spit up on his suit jacket. Not that Congressman Raymond McKenna seemed to mind.

"Hey, Grandpa, you got some on you," Aileen teased, handing him a towel.

"It's a price I'm glad to pay to have this little

one in my arms." He winked at her. "I'll be looking forward to your first baby, too."

Raymond glanced over at Rhys, who was watching football on the big screen with Donovan and Skelly. Football on Christmas Eve. Even a man who was half wolf got sucked in to the male bonding sport.

Aileen grinned. "Don't get ahead of yourself."

She did want kids and she knew Rhys did, as well, but first they had to work out their relationship. And she needed to finish her thesis and find a job or get a grant that would allow her to work from Wolf Creek. One day, whatever they needed to do to manage it, she was convinced they would have a family of their own. For now, she was happy just knowing that Rhys wanted to be with her as much as she wanted to be with him.

Aileen kissed her father on the cheek as Laurel rushed by, heading for the front door and announcing, "New arrivals!"

A commercial break in the game released the men to get up and welcome the incoming guests.

Rhys drifted to Aileen's side and nuzzled her neck. "Donovan and I talked," he murmured. "Things at the DNR are going as we hoped. Everyone seems satisfied the wolf problem is taken care of."

"Thank goodness." Aileen moved in closer to

him. She couldn't get enough of Rhys. "Now let's hope it's true."

"You're still worried about Caine?"

"Aren't you?"

"I don't like him, but I don't think he's another Magnus. I'll keep an eye on him just in case."

The best they could do at the moment. Assuming Caine was another werewolf...then, again, that didn't mean he had to be evil. Aileen didn't want more trouble, so she was going to manifest their being done with trouble for now.

She pulled Rhys to the newcomers at the door. "This is my cousin, Keelin, her husband, Tyler, their daughters, Cheryl and Kelly."

"Ah, Rhys, good to be meeting you in person," Keelin said, her gray eyes searching his face.

"In person?"

"Well, I've been seeing you in my dreams."

The Irish lilt to her voice made that sound pleasant, but Aileen knew she'd been privy to their terror on the solstice.

"Keelin and I have a lot in common," Aileen told Rhys. She and her cousin had a lot to talk about. Now that Aileen had decided to tune up her gift, she could use any tips Keelin could give her. "I'll explain later."

"Fine by me. Do you mind?" Rhys asked, indicating the television. The commercials were ended and the men were already drifting back to watch the game, Tyler with them.

"Go," she said, pushing him, pleased that he fit in so well with her brothers.

She turned back to Keelin in time to see the expression her cousin tried to cover. "What? Is something wrong?"

"It's Flanna," she said of her younger sister, who lived in Ireland. "I've been seeing her in my dreams, as well."

"And?"

"It's probably nothing. Something about this jewelry collection she's working on. I've a bad feeling that it will bring her trouble is all."

Flanna was a talented jewelry designer who hadn't yet gotten the recognition she deserved.

"Have you tried calling her?"

"Aye, this morning. She says everything is fine and told me not to be a goose."

"Then don't be a goose. Just eat some, because that's what Laurel has in the oven."

The cousins laughed together and Aileen's positive mood was restored. Keelin went off to help Laurel, but Aileen stayed put for a moment and gave thanks for the way things with the werewolf situation had ended. Gave thanks for the family she loved dearly. Gave thanks for Rhys.

Everything seemed better and brighter this

evening. She inhaled and the pine smelled more intense, the spices coming from the kitchen smelled more exotic. She saw details about Donovan's home she hadn't noticed the last time she'd been here—the subtle wolf etchings in the fireplace mantle, the cast of a wolf's paw on a far shelf the same color as the pale wall behind it. She heard laughter coming from another room. And an icicle dropping from the eaves outside. All her senses were sharper, more in tune with her surroundings.

Suddenly coming up behind her and wrapping a possessive arm around her waist, Rhys asked, "What's going on in that beautiful head of yours?"

"I was just thinking of how much I love you." She turned in his arms and teased, "And about the present I got you for Christmas."

"I already got the best Christmas present ever," he said, brushing his lips across hers. "You're more than any man could wish for."

And he was more than she could ever have imagined—Gran's legacy come true.

* * * * *

Coming from The McKenna Legacy—
Flanna's story.

*Look for IN NAME ONLY, coming soon
in the next installment of*
THE McKENNA LEGACY
*from Patricia Rosemoor
and Harlequin Intrigue.*

Kimberley Blackstone didn't notice the waiting horde of media until it was too late. Flashbulbs exploded around her like a New Year's light show. She skidded to a halt, so abruptly her trailing suitcase all but overtook her.

This had to be a case of mistaken identity. Surely. Kimberley hadn't been on the paparazzi hit list for close to a decade, not since she'd estranged herself from her billionaire father and his headline-hungry diamond business.

But no, it was *her* name they called. *Her* face was the focus of a swarm of lenses that circled her like avid hornets. Her heart started to pound with fear-fueled adrenaline.

What did they want?

What was going on?

With a rising sense of bewilderment she scanned the crowd for a clue, and her gaze fastened on a tall, leonine figure forcing his way to the front. A tall, familiar figure. Her head came up in stunned recognition, and their gazes collided across the sea of heads before the cameras erupted with another barrage of flashes, this time right in her exposed face.

Blinded by the flashbulbs—and by the shock of that momentary eye-meet—Kimberley didn't realize his intent until he'd forged his way to her side, possibly by the sheer strength of his personality. She felt his arm wrap around her shoulder, pulling her into the protective shelter of his body, allowing her no time to object. No chance to lift her hands to ward him off.

In the space of a hastily drawn breath, she found herself plastered knee-to-nose against six feet two inches of hard-bodied male.

Ric Perrini.

Her lover for ten torrid weeks, her husband for ten tumultuous days.

Her ex for ten tranquil years.

After all this time, he should not have felt so

familiar but, oh dear, he did. She knew the scent of that body and its lean, muscular strength. She knew its heat and its slick power and every response it could draw from hers.

She also recognized the ease with which he'd taken control of the moment and the decisiveness of his deep voice when it rumbled close to her ear. "I have a car waiting outside. Is this your only luggage?"

Kimberley nodded. "I assume you will tell me," she said tightly, "what this welcome party is all about."

"Not while the welcome party is within earshot. No."

Barking a request for the cameramen to stand aside, Perrini took her hand and pulled her into step with his ground-eating stride. Kimberley let him, because he was right, damn his arrogant, Italian-suited hide. Despite the speed with which he whisked her across the airport terminal, she could almost feel the hot breath of the pursuing media on her back.

This was neither the time nor the place for explanations. Inside his car, however, she would get answers.

Now that the initial shock had been blown away—by the haste of their retreat, by the heat of her gathering indignation, by the rush of adrenaline fired by Perrini's presence and the looming verbal battle—her brain was starting to tick over. This had to be her father's doing. And if it was a Howard Blackstone publicity ploy, then it had to be about Blackstone Diamonds, the company that ruled his life.

The knowledge made her chest tighten with a familiar ache of disillusionment.

She'd known her father would be flying in from Sydney for today's opening of the newest in his chain of exclusive, high-end jewelry boutiques. The opulent shop front sat adjacent to the rival business where Kimberley worked. No coincidence, she thought bitterly, just as it was no coincidence that Ric Perrini was here in Auckland ushering her to his car.

Perrini was Howard Blackstone's right-hand man, second in command at Blackstone Diamonds, a legacy of his short-lived marriage to the boss's daughter. No doubt her father had sent him to fetch her; the question was *why?*

* * * * *

Get swept away down under with the glitz and glamour of the Blackstone empire as Kimberley tries to determine the real reason behind her "reunion" with Ric....

Look for VOWS & A VENGEFUL GROOM
by Bronwyn Jameson,
in stores January 2008.

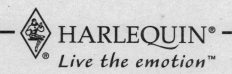

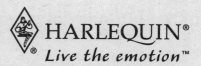

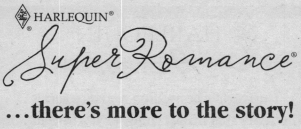

HARLEQUIN®

Super Romance®

...there's more to the story!

Superromance.
A *big* satisfying read about unforgettable
characters. Each month we offer *six* very different
stories that range from family drama to adventure
and mystery, from highly emotional stories to
romantic comedies—and much more! Stories
about people you'll believe in and care about.
Stories too compelling to put down....

Our authors are among today's *best* romance
writers. You'll find familiar names and talented
newcomers. Many of them are award winners—
and you'll see why!

If you want the biggest and best
in romance fiction, you'll get it
from Superromance!

Exciting, Emotional, Unexpected...

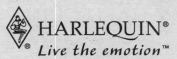

HARLEQUIN®
Live the emotion™

HSDIR06

HARLEQUIN®
Presents®

The world's bestselling romance series...
The series that brings you your favorite authors,
month after month:

Helen Bianchin...Emma Darcy
Lynne Graham...Penny Jordan
Miranda Lee...Sandra Marton
Anne Mather...Carole Mortimer
Susan Napier...Michelle Reid

and many more uniquely talented authors!

Wealthy, powerful, gorgeous men...
Women who have feelings just like your own...
The stories you love; set in exotic, glamorous locations...

HARLEQUIN®
Presents®

Seduction and Passion Guaranteed!

HPDIR104

Harlequin® Historical
Historical Romantic Adventure!

*Imagine a time of chivalrous
knights and unconventional ladies,
roguish rakes and impetuous
heiresses, rugged cowboys
and spirited frontierswomen—
these rich and vivid tales will
capture your imagination!*

*Harlequin Historical . . .
they're too good to miss!*

HHDIR06

SPECIAL EDITION™

Emotional, compelling stories that capture the intensity of
living, loving and creating a family in today's world.

Desire

Modern, passionate reads that are powerful and provocative.

nocturne

Dramatic and sensual tales of paranormal romance.

Romantic SUSPENSE

Romances that are sparked by danger and fueled by passion.